Punch Line

JOEY SLINGER

KEY PORTER  BOOKS

Library and Archives Canada Cataloguing in Publication
Slinger, Joey
   Punch line / Joey Slinger.

ISBN 1-55263-697-6

I. Title.

PS8587.L5P95   2005   C813'.6   C2005-902646-4

The publisher gratefully acknowledges the support of the Canada Council for the Arts and the Ontario Arts Council for its publishing program. We acknowledge the support of the Government of Ontario through the Ontario Media Development Corporation's Ontario Book Initiative.

We acknowledge the financial support of the Government of Canada through the Book Publishing Industry Development Program (BPIDP) for our publishing activities.

Key Porter Books Limited
Six Adelaide Street East, Tenth Floor
Toronto, Ontario
Canada M5C 1H6

www.keyporter.com

Text design: Peter Maher
Electronic formatting: Jean Lightfoot Peters

Printed and bound in Canada

05 06 07 08 09 5 4 3 2 1

Punch Line

To Yankel,
who done it.

o n e

IT QUICKLY BECAME OBVIOUS that Ballantine missed his wife in a terrible way. No sooner had a decent interval of mourning passed than he began making plans to track down and kill the three assholes who had scared her to death. For a man who was eighty-one years old and who, as far as he could remember, had never caused even the slightest physical harm to any other human being, a murder spree took him into realms beyond any he had ever imagined, but by the time he had worked out that he could kill a nineteen-year-old asshole and that he could live with it, actually doing it became almost tedious. Later on he came to suspect he chose bungee cord as a murder weapon just to make it interesting. He could always just have come up behind the assholes and whacked them over the head five or six times with a jack handle.

Bungee jumping seemed to pop into everybody's conversation back then, so it wasn't exactly an idea out of left field, but having fastened on to it, he then faced the first of some really tough questions. How do you knock somebody off with bungee cord? Other than strangling them, that is. Strangling with any kind of material would likely involve a struggle, and Ballantine figured he wouldn't have a chance against a smallish seven-year-old girl in a struggle much less an apprentice welder the size of a Toyota. And anyway, strangling wouldn't express the essential nature of his chosen murder weapon, namely its bungee-ness.

He could hardly go around asking people for hypothetical suggestions because when it happened—especially since it was going to happen three times—they might start to think maybe the question hadn't been entirely hypothetical. Besides that, he couldn't think of anybody he'd care to ask. For all practical purposes, and for the first time in his life, he was completely on his own. When he was knocking off the first two assholes he sometimes wondered if he was doing it because he resented being on his own, but when he finally moved into The Cloister and wasn't that much on his own any more, he found that he became even more interested in knocking people off.

At first, though, he'd just been pissed off because his wife had been scared to death. It had taken awhile to locate the assholes who had done it, but he hadn't been in a rush. Why would he have been? He didn't have anything else to do. Not having anything to do had been driving him crazy, but when he came up with something and it turned out to be murdering the assholes with bungee cord it drove him even crazier. Everybody he discussed it with afterward—and when he started living in The Cloister he was surprised to discover it was the sort of thing people cared to discuss a lot—said it would drive anybody crazy. How do you get a great big asshole fastened to the end of a bungee cord? And then what do you do with him? So you slice the cord and he plummets to his death. Big deal. And what does he plummet from? How do you get him to the "what" from which he plummets?

Here, sir. Try this chair. It's an extra-comfy new design. Just sit down and give it a whirl. Go ahead, you are under no obligation. Lean back. There. How's it feel?

Pulls lever.

Whoosh!

It was a very difficult thing to picture. He started scouting sites. A bridge would probably be good—launch the asshole over the railing into the river. That was when he tripped over the problem that had concerned so many other players in the great game of justice dispensing. Collateral damage. Usually it was spoken of in tones of mild regret, or sarcastically. But even a slight possibility of wiping out an innocent bicyclist on the path beside the river when Asshole No. 1, perhaps as a result of the wind, perhaps as a result of miscalculation, came flying over the railing forty-five degrees off course filled Ballantine's intestines with icy dread. Yet thinking about a clean shot—dreaming of a perfect trajectory, the optimum launch velocity, the flailing arms, the trailing legs, the cry of terror, the distant splash—poked a little hole of joy in his pain as he sat night after night missing his wife.

Then one day an amazing thing happened.

He was scouting sites near where Asshole No. 1 lived, trying out some larger-scale and smaller-scale approaches with no precise design to any of them. He was jacking around, as he would admit much later, but with an air of purpose that made him feel as if he was accomplishing something. Eliminating ideas that were really, really stupid. He tied one end of a long piece of bungee cord as big around as his thumb to a rusted pipe that had once been used to fill the oil tanks in the building the asshole lived in with his mother. He knotted the other end to a grille that had more teeth kicked out of it than were left and supposedly kept intruders from getting through the basement window of the building next door. He took hold of the middle of the cord with both hands and, stepping backwards, stretched it down the narrow alley between the buildings, worrying more and more, as the tension increased, about the broken wine bottles and discarded automobile tires under foot. He was concentrating intensely on staying upright when he heard something and looked up—and there was Asshole No. 1 walking toward him. He was just crossing into the shadow of the alleyway from the bright daylight of the street. He moved so deliberately it was as if they had an appointment and here he was.

But instead of coming up to Ballantine and beating the shit out of him, or even coming up to him and screaming in his face and Ballantine ending up being scared to death pretty much the way his wife had been, he opened his fly and took a piss against the wall. No sneering glances, no obscene gestures. Was it possible he didn't even notice Ballantine standing there? It was all so unexpected that Ballantine had a powerful urge to run like hell in the opposite direction. Much later, of course, the legend would attribute this to opening-night jitters, but now, as he tried to get his nerves under control, he shifted his stance and stepped on one of the puke-drenched slabs of cardboard the rubbies slept on, which was about as close as he could come to stepping on a thousand ball bearings. For reasons he could never figure out, he kept hold of the bungee cord, and now it whipped him forward so rapidly he was parallel to the ground when his head smashed into Asshole No. 1's kidney. Ballantine was never sure whether Asshole No. 1 swore or just squealed in pain, but he made some kind of awful noise, then reeled like a bowling pin out of the alleyway, across the sidewalk, off the curb, and in front of the bus that was pulling away from the stop outside his building.

Ballantine skidded to a landing on his chin, and opened his eyes just in time to see the right front wheel of the bus clump very slightly as it crushed Asshole No. 1's chest.

He stood for a moment, trembling beside the legs that were sticking out from under the bus, his mind not yet able to put together what had happened. It was then that he began learning the first of the two lessons that would guide him through all his future efforts, although its full importance wouldn't be clear for some time. It was this: Nobody looked at him. And if they did, they didn't notice him. Nobody pointed him out as having had something to do with the horrible accident. The bus driver even bumped into him, knocking him aside after examining the bloody mulch behind the right front wheel and turning to climb back on board to trip the signal that would bring emergency crews. It was as if Ballantine wasn't there at all. The second lesson was obvious by the time he pushed through the growing cluster of people and hurried away, and was a reinforcement, thanks to what had just happened, of something he had believed pretty much his entire life. It was this: Careful planning and attention to detail—they pay off.

t w o

BALLANTINE SPENT SEVERAL WEEKS shadowing Asshole No. 2, during which time he witnessed some extraordinary things, especially the funeral service for Asshole No. 1. When the police broke down the door of the funeral home and slammed the coffin lid shut and rounded up exactly the same mourners who, when they paid their respects before the service began, had dropped mementoes into the coffin, Ballantine was surprised. He obviously wasn't the only one keeping the proceedings under surveillance, and the mental note he made would come in handy when the executive committee at The Cloister needed ways to get rid of evidence, and departed guests ended up carrying more than their own secrets to the grave.

"Ya cocksuckers!" was what the mother of Asshole No. 1 kept shouting as she made jack-off gestures at the police when they carried her late son out of the funeral home. Asshole No. 2 was not, as things turned out, among those taken into custody.

This didn't surprise Ballantine because Asshole No. 2 hadn't been at the funeral. He had been banging Asshole No. 1's grieving girlfriend in Asshole No. 1's mother's apartment, where the girlfriend had gone in search of the money she was sure Asshole No. 1 had been hiding from her. This was also what Asshole No. 2 had gone to look for when their encounter filled the air with romance.

Ballantine, naturally, was not able to be at the funeral and on the fire escape watching Asshole No. 2's pimply ass hammer away between the late Asshole No. 1's girl-friend's knees. He had left a cash payment with the funeral director for a videotape of the service, one of the many remembrance options available to grieving parties, which was mailed to him in due course. The scene out-side the funeral home, with the coffin being loaded into a police van rather than the hearse, and the arrested mourners being loaded into another one, was on the news that night. It was the first time Asshole No. 1 had ever been mentioned by the media. The actions that caused him to be murdered, and were soon to have the same effect on Asshole No. 2, were neither newsworthy nor even noticed by anyone other than Ballantine and his late wife when they had scared her to death.

Ballantine didn't realize that he was about to become a legendary serial killer at a time of life when most people weren't about to become anything except gaga or dead. What he did realize was that the task he had set himself would never be completed if he had to take care of all the administrative details, such as doing his laun-dry and buying TV dinners and putting them in the oven and discovering two hours later that he hadn't turned it on. He needed a support system, and that was why he arranged to move into The Cloister, a residential facility.

As for the murderous binge he had committed him-self to, which he imagined would come to an end with three dead assholes, he felt a businesslike satisfaction about it. He would have stopped if the circumstances had been different. And he would never use bungee cord again. Carrying out the murders, he calculated, took two years longer than it ought to have because he insisted on bungee cord being the fatal weapon, although by the end hardly anybody thought about bungee any more—either bungee jumping or bungee cord, except for the light-weight kind you use to hold down stuff you drive around with on the roof of the car. For awhile there, though, it had been on the news every day. People bungee jumping from bridges. From helicopters. At amusement parks where they paid to jump off spindly scaffolding ten storeys high. Pitching down like hanged men, except hanged by the ankles. Then—*DOINK!*—yanked back up. Then down again. Up and down, up and down, until the cord was all bounced out. It was most newsworthy when a cord broke. Or when the cord parted on the rebound, catapulting the jumper into the sky like a rock from a slingshot. But even without a cord breaking, and without a fatality or a crippling injury, it was still a news-hour favourite. Crazy people! What they won't do for a thrill. Here's two of them getting married while they bungee jump. It made good visuals.

When guns first appeared, they stayed in use. They became a fixture on the premeditated murder scene. It was the same with knives. But bungee cord, which made its appearance as a murder weapon when Ballantine introduced it, disappeared as a murder weapon the minute he quit using it. For a long time he envied murderers who kept it simple, who just burst in and blasted away. Wasn't the objective the "what"—killing three assholes—not the "how"? But here he was, bogged down in developing a *modus operandi* as they called it on television. An M.O. As they used to call it on television anyway. Now, as far as he could tell, they just said, "the way the murderer keeps fucking doing it." Shouldn't he have been coming up with different ways of doing it so it wouldn't be obvious that his murders were connected? That's when it crossed his mind that what he should have been doing had never really crossed his mind. He felt as if he was just a passenger in a body that was doing this and that, and he rarely encountered whoever was driving. For that reason, sudden route changes or unexpected destinations didn't surprise him. It wasn't even clear that he noticed when they happened.

He definitely didn't notice that when he moved into The Cloister he became an immediate media sensation. The big hungry maw of the media in The Cloister always needed feeding even if pretty much the only thing the media consisted of was "News & Views Roundup," produced, directed, and anchored by Mt. Rushmore. "News & Views Roundup" became a staple the day Mt. Rushmore moved in and discovered that nobody had ever bothered to unpack the video camera the social committee had acquired, much less arranged for Speed to hook it into The Cloister's closed-circuit cable system. For no reason other than the idea came to him when he found a big old fake oil painting of Mt. Rushmore in the craft-therapy locker, he'd opened that first night with an eye-catching graphic he'd made by cutting out photographs of his own face and gluing them over the mountain's monumental ones. It would become his and the show's trademark: A historic broadcaster and broadcasting history were born at the same moment.

Nevertheless, Mt. Rushmore did claim genuine journalism credentials, having for many years operated a cigar store that had a newsstand. This was back when cigars hadn't become the Mark of Satan, as he always put it, and magazines contained information other than the size of the tits in the accompanying photograph.

He wasn't alone in the journalistic field. Management had a channel that listed events scheduled for each day, and on the print end there was the management newsletter that nobody read other than relatives of guests who seemed to believe it was their responsibility to know about upcoming in-house seminars on "New approaches to the installation of catheters." Every now and then some social-climbing new arrival would come out with a social notes publication, but these almost always fizzled because the social notes and gossip other guests passed along to her—it was always a her—were entirely made up, which everybody else knew and the novice publisher soon discovered and, as a result, shut the operation down to put an end to the ridicule.

This wasn't a problem with "News & Views Roundup" since the news was whatever Mt. Rushmore decided it was, and the views were whatever he happened to hold at the time, and they were rounded up in a way that people assumed must have made some sense to somebody even if it didn't to them. Not that anybody much watched, although The Cloister's attendants did find that when they parked the gagas in front of the screen and turned on Mt. Rushmore's show, which was in the pre-dinner time slot, the sight of his big flubbery face jabbering away, even with the sound turned right down, calmed them, making it easier to spoon their food into them and minimizing the hosing down needed afterward.

Feeding that monstrous media maw was a challenge, and Mt. Rushmore was constantly on the lookout for any of The Cloister's guests he might interview. He had already profiled all the long-standing guests, and every one of them refused to come on again because Mt. Rushmore's devious efforts to trick them into saying something honest about The Cloister's management made them nervous. So he was reduced to picking off the newcomers, which he tempted by saying it was a wonderful way for their fellow guests to get to know them.

Ballantine struck him right off as a fabulous prospect. There was the mysterious canvas-covered bundle that was so heavy the attendants grumbled about having to get a dolly to move it into his room. There was the way he was always coming and going, always jumping up from the table as soon as he finished eating and hurrying out of the dining room, and often out of the building. Often for hours. He seemed friendly enough, but he never wandered into the sunrooms or the Evening Cookie Club looking to hear somebody's life story or to tell somebody his. He seemed entirely self-contained, but also self-possessed, although not in a way that was off-putting. Mt. Rushmore decided it was more the way professional athletes are self-possessed when they prepare for an important game. They are focused on something other than this moment, they are putting on their game faces and whatever you are interrupting them with is a distraction, although Ballantine was cheerful enough when Mt. Rushmore encountered him, which he did by leaping in front of him whenever he could and forcing him to make eye contact and exchange some kind of greeting. In fact, he was cheerful as could be. That was the weirdest thing, as far as Mt. Rushmore was concerned. Not just cheerful, this new guest seemed downright happy. And nobody who arrived in The Cloister was all that happy right off the bat. If they got happier over time, it was a grudging happiness. This was not a place any of them genuinely imagined they would end up. They believed that if they managed to stay alive, they would somehow be spared this. Becoming a guest at The Cloister did not fill them with happiness unless they were nuts.

There were lots of gagas in The Cloister, but only because they required less attention and effort than the guests who were compos and mentis and could feed themselves and take themselves to the bathroom and wipe their own asses, and remember to pull their trousers up or their skirts down before they came back out. Nuts, on the other hand, caused no end of trouble. There was no telling what they might do next, and there were residential facilities that specialized in caring for them where, if they wanted to wreck the place, they could be strapped into straitjackets and drugged into stupors. That went beyond the mandate of The Cloister, to the great disappointment of Dixon, the chief administrator, and her team, who felt that certain control mechanisms they were denied would permit them to run an even more efficient operation even if none of the guests was going berserk and wrecking the place.

If Ballantine was as happy as he appeared to be, it could mean he was nuts, and if he was nuts, Mt. Rushmore definitely wanted him on "News & Views Roundup" because it would be easier to trick a nut into saying the things about management that Mt. Rushmore always hoped one of his on-camera guests would say. But he would have to move quickly because it wouldn't be long before Dixon noticed Ballantine and had him hogtied and hauled off to a more suitable setting, with locked wards and electroconvulsive therapy available around the clock.

Mt. Rushmore became even more determined when Ballantine kept making excuses for not being available to appear on the show. It interfered with his schedule, he apologized. This astounded Mt. Rushmore. Everybody in The Cloister had their own schedule, but all the schedules were exactly the same. Management went to enormous lengths to make sure they were. And this didn't interfere with their availability to appear on his show. The only thing that interfered with their availability to appear on his show was that they didn't want to appear on his show. But Ballantine had never been on television before and thought it would be an interesting experience. His problem was scheduling.

"He must be nuts if he thinks he's got some other kind of schedule," Mt. Rushmore said to Sister Bernice as they sat around after lunch waiting to be shooed away from their table and out of the dining room.

Sister Bernice nodded. "Cuckoo City."

"The *mayor* of Cuckoo City!" chirped Banana, who was always lurking around, waiting to jump in with a punch line or to improve the punch line of whoever jumped in with one ahead of him.

Sister Bernice and Mt. Rushmore swivelled and stared at him. Banana smiled helpfully. "Cuckoo City is ordinary crazy," he explained, as he always did when people didn't quite get his punch lines or understand why his improvement made theirs better. "That's the way everybody in Cuckoo City is. But the mayor is, like, really, *really* crazy. That's why they elected him. This new guy sounds like he'd definitely be a candidate," Banana said. "For mayor."

Sister Bernice and Mt. Rushmore looked at their watches and decided it wasn't worth waiting to be shooed out of the dining room, even though it was something they enjoyed because it sharpened the little edge of irritation provoked by management's emphatic claim that The Cloister was their home and they were welcome to live in it as they would have in the actual homes they had lived in before.

Word got around. Not only that this new guest had some weird schedule that conflicted with Mt. Rushmore's showtimes, but also, as many other guests started to notice, that he was peculiarly busy, and happy, and self-contained. But polite. Pleasant. Cheerful. Cheerful as could be.

Cuckoo City.

The result was that when Ballantine finally did find an opportunity and was booked to appear, the show got the biggest ratings in its history. Speed, who had an electronic measuring device, was able to inform Mt. Rushmore afterwards that fourteen sets had been tuned in, although it was impossible to say how many of these had the sound turned all the way down. And since one of these sets was in a sunroom, where a crowd always gathered in anticipation of the dinner chime, Mt. Rushmore confidently estimated that Ballantine's appearance had been seen, if not heard, by as many as twenty or even twenty-five guests.

Ballantine was nervous at first. He was surprised by how tiny the TV camera was, and he tried to avoid looking at himself in the monitor because it made him feel shy. What was *he* of all people doing on *television*? But he forgot all about it when Mt. Rushmore started asking his questions. There was something about Mt. Rushmore that made him feel wonderfully, peacefully comfortable.

"Well," he replied, after a few of the essential details had been extracted—widower, eighty-two, two daughters, one an orthodontist, three grandchildren, wholesale fruits and vegetables until he retired at seventy-one—"I picked The Cloister because they had a room coming available—"

"They do have a way of becoming available," interjected the host.

"—and I needed a place where my basic needs could be satisfied, like, you know, meals and somebody to keep the place clean, while I carried out some long-term plans."

"Long-term plans?" Mt. Rushmore saw a news angle and leapt on it. "Could you tell us what those are?"

"Sure. My wife was scared to death by three assholes on the subway one night when we were riding home after a movie. After she died, I decided to murder them."

Nuts as can be, thought Mt. Rushmore. "Oh, really?" he said, his eyes widening.

But his "Oh, really?" was unnecessary. He didn't have to say anything or ask anything, although he did from time to time stare directly into the camera with an "Uh-oh, what have we here?" look on his face.

All he had to do was let Ballantine roll on. Ballantine found it was a very pleasant thing to do, sit in this room with this other old guy and explain what he'd been up to. He'd been up to a lot, but something was missing. He'd had no outlet, no one to share it with. It had been building up in him, and while he didn't want to make it into some kind of big deal, he was proud of it and appreciated the—although Mt. Rushmore didn't come right out and say it—commendation he detected in the TV host's eyes.

Whatever the look in Mt. Rushmore's eyes was, it wasn't commendation. His brain was whirling like mad. There is, he was thinking, something really strange about this nut. And the strangeness was this: He didn't sound nuts. He didn't sound any more nuts than the taxi drivers who would stop in Mt. Rushmore's cigar store to buy Tums and tell him about a couple of peculiar fares they'd had that morning.

The details were detailed, but not screwy detailed, not detailed in some obsessive, pathological way. They were just the sort of details a person working on a big project might pass along to an interested layman.

By the time the Ballantine interview segment was over, all Mt. Rushmore could manage to say was, "Bungee cord?!" over and over. And when the show itself was over he hurried out and caught up to Ballantine in the lineup for the dining room and said, "That was—that was—that was—really interesting."

"Thanks," said Ballantine. "It was really interesting being on TV."

"Don't worry, probably nobody was watching." Mt Rushmore said this in a way that might have soothed someone who needed soothing. But Ballantine didn't.

"I just mean it was a whole new experience for me."

"Listen, you were good. Really good. A natural."

Ballantine smiled and let his head droop modestly. Although it was enjoyable, he would have let this pass as schmoozy TV-host bullshit except that Mt. Rushmore leaned in close to his ear.

"That stuff you said about those guys, those—"

"Assholes?" said Ballantine helpfully.

"Yeah. Was that all"—he looked around to make sure no one else could hear—"was that true?"

"Oh, yeah." Ballantine didn't sound even slightly offended. "I could show you the—"

"No! No! Listen!" The chime chimed, the doors swung open and the line started shuffling forward. "There's some people I'd like to meet you."

"Geez. I don't want to be...you know. But I've got a lot of things—"

"To do?"

"—to do. Exactly."

"That's why I want them to meet you."

three

AND WHAT DID THAT LEAD TO? It led to this: The
creation of The Cloister's guests' executive committee,
which was accomplished by changing the name of The
Cloister's guests' social and recreation committee. Its membership, like that of the social and recreation committee,
was made up of anybody who showed up at the meetings.

And it led to this: Ballantine was dying.

This put him in a very difficult spot. Unless he actually died. If he actually died, it wouldn't make any
difference one way or the other. But if he didn't, it would
make all the difference in the world.

If he didn't die, he was dead.

"I'm dead," he croaked to Mt. Rushmore as he was
being wheeled out of his room.

"It's just a cold," Mt. Rushmore said soothingly. Mt.
Rushmore had come along to comfort him.

He wasn't doing a very good job. "Maybe it will get
worse," said Ballantine. "Maybe it's already worse. Maybe
it's pneumonia."

Mt. Rushmore couldn't help but hear the ragged note
of hope. "You're right." He patted Ballantine's shoulder.
"It could be a little pneumonia."

With pneumonia you could at least really die. Your
lungs could fill up, drowning you in your own fluids. You
could be gone by midnight. For an exhilarating second,
Ballantine thought this could be his last day on earth.

He looked at Mt. Rushmore, who was studiously watching the red numbers above the elevator door. Away on either side stretched the corridor that was so slickly polished the *sritch, sritch* of the rubber-soled shoes the attendants and practical nurses wore could be heard coming from the other end of the building. Nobody was passing by, though. No guests, no staff. No other witnesses.

A little pneumonia! Ballantine wanted to cheer.

Except shouldn't he be wheezing? Shouldn't he have a temperature? Shouldn't he feel weak and, you know, weaker than this? Shouldn't he feel sick? Not that he didn't feel sick. He felt like absolute shit. But not sick sick. Just feel-like-absolute-shit sick. Like he was going to die. He knew that feeling. Everybody knew that feeling.

He groaned.

"No," he said. "It's just a cold."

The attendants glared at the disgusting old fuck on the gurney. They would happily have pummelled him black and blue and wheeled him away, bleeding from the nose and the ears. Or pried the elevator doors open and pushed him into the empty shaft. They would happily have hurt the old fuck as much as they possibly could because of the disruption he had caused to the efficient operation of The Cloister and for the threat he presented to their own well-being. Except they couldn't do anything but feign their customary indifference and carry out their assigned task because there was his old fuck of a pal standing beside him, taking it all in. So they, too, raised their eyes, focusing their loathing on the red numbers above the elevator door.

"I can't believe they tracked you down," Mt. Rushmore whispered, never glancing away from the flickering numbers until they slowed and stopped and the doors slid open.

Tracked him down, captured him, sentenced him to death, because once they rolled him off the elevator at the Concourse level and along to the loading dock, he would never be allowed back into The Cloister. Once you were out, you were out, and if he was out, he wouldn't be able to do one or two very important things that desperately needed doing. This would kill him. That's why he'd gone into hiding the minute he'd gotten a sniffle. For three days he'd been on the run. His constant moving to avoid detection sometimes made it difficult for the executive committee to find him and slip him food. The executive committee didn't want him to die until he'd done the things that needed doing either.

Most people took it for granted that the guests in The Cloister were dying. Ballantine took it for granted that he was, and that he had been since the day he was born. That was okay with him, generally speaking. It was absolutely wonderful as far as The Cloister was concerned. Guests died all the time, and its efficient system swung into operation the minute they did. The room was sprayed with antiseptic, the bedclothes were changed, the next of kin were notified, and the departed guest was wheeled down to the loading dock at the back of the building and hauled away by one of the hearses that were always there waiting with their motors running. By this time a new guest had been installed in the room.

Maintaining maximum capacity was something The Cloister took great pride in. That was why it had a policy of zero tolerance when it came to colds. Anybody could get sick, this was an actuarially sound assumption. When a guest got sick, there were two possibilities—they would get better or they would die. If they got better, they got better. And while they were sick their costs per diem decreased because they consumed much less food than they did when they were well. If they died, they died. The staff was trained to deal with death. They worked happily in the midst of it every day, and unless they were on duty when the end came and they were obliged to change the sheets, the transition to a new guest was seamless and often unnoticeable, especially if the new guest kept the photographs of the departed guest's family on the dresser, possibly because they didn't have any family of their own, and left the same grandchildren's drawings taped to the walls, and wore the former guest's clothing, possibly because their own had been lost in transit. Often the staff received commendations for how quickly they could spray the room with antiseptic, change the sheets, and roll the departed guest down to the loading dock where the first hearse in line would squeal its wheels as it roared out of the rank. By the time the attendants returned from the loading dock, the new guest had settled in and the staff went busily about the task of waiting for the newcomer to die and making sure that nothing interrupted that process.

Fortunately, none of the sicknesses the guests died from were sicknesses the staff could easily catch, if you discount salmonella, which flared up no more often than could be expected in an institution where expenditures on food were a substantial part of the budget and could easily be controlled through careful purchasing. Their other sicknesses were the sicknesses of old people. Except for colds. Anybody could catch a cold and that's why the policy was zero tolerance. A guest with a cold might pass it along to a staff member from whom fellow staff members might catch it. The operation of The Cloister, which depended on minimum staffing for maximum capacity, would falter. Because they risked passing it on to other staff members, employees with colds weren't allowed to come to work. And when they couldn't work, they didn't get paid. And that was why there was nothing worse that could happen to a guest than catch one.

If you caught one, they sent you to the hospital.

"In the hospital there's no telling what you might catch," Mt. Rushmore said, something Ballantine knew full well. Another thing he knew full well was that whether you did or didn't catch something in the hospital, you never came back to The Cloister. You could apply for readmission, but gaining it was out of the question because your file had been stamped "Not Suitable" under the entry that said you were the sort of person who caught colds.

Guests often said things that other guests knew full well because the guest who said it had told them the same thing five minutes earlier, and possibly a number of times before that. Mt. Rushmore, however, wasn't saying something Ballantine knew full well just to make conversation. Ballantine knew this full well, too. Mt. Rushmore was saying it because it was the sort of thing friends who came along to comfort guests being shipped off to hospital always said, and because it would keep the attendants off their guard. It was important that the attendants treat this hospital transfer no differently than any other even though they knew full well that this shipment was different. This was why they wished they could beat the old fuck on the gurney senseless.

Ballantine was Number One on Dixon's Troublemakers List, and the babbling old fuck who was tagging along was Number Two. There were barely a dozen guests on the Troublemakers List and the staff kept careful track of them. For instance, they knew that the canvas-wrapped coil of heavy-duty bungee cord that was among Ballantine's belongings when he moved into The Cloister had disappeared some months afterward. And they knew that until he became a guest, there hadn't been a Troublemakers List or any reason to compile one. Now there were very good reasons, and a staff member who could find an excuse to ship one of the troublemakers out was regarded highly by Dixon and her management team. It genuinely troubled Dixon to think that any guest would make trouble for her, and Ballantine was the first one ever to do so. The trouble he caused was this: Not long after he showed up, other guests began to cause trouble. The guests' executive committee concluded that Dixon believed getting rid of any of the guests on the Troublemakers List would make things better, but that getting rid of Ballantine would make things perfect because once he was gone, none of the other guests on the list would make any more trouble. This was why the executive committee felt it was particularly important to keep Ballantine from being sent to hospital.

Besides, Ballantine would be far better off in The Cloister than in a hospital, and not just for the obvious reason that in The Cloister he was less likely to catch some fatal disease. While the roster varied, the list of guests living in The Cloister at any given time tended to include a wider variety of medical specialists than any hospital had, and far more registered nurses, physiotherapists, weapons experts, and individuals with exceptional skills in manufacturing explosive devices and acquiring the materials necessary to do so.

The executive committee's position on medical care on the outside was summarized by Sister Bernice in a briefing she gave on the limits of treatment. "Any doctor who recommends exploratory surgery or a CAT-scan for any of the guests here is a charlatan since we are all going to die before long anyway." Wisdom aside, the committee had no power—all it could do was offer advice, and there were always guests who couldn't keep from going along with a doctor's recommendations, and were taken away to a clinic for tests or a scan and were never seen again.

That's why colds were such a frightening proposition. There was no treatment. There was no disguising the symptoms. "Your nose can run, but it can't hide," guests murmured apprehensively.

And it wasn't as if Ballantine could hop off the gurney and grab one of the off-the-books, non-resident stiffs Fastrack had been stacking so brazenly on the loading dock and send it off to the hospital in his place. Management had been on to that dodge for some time now. It was why Dixon insisted two attendants accompany every hospital transfer all the way to the ambulance, and why ambulance attendants were required to sign a form stating the guest still showed some vital signs when it was picked up. Because it was Ballantine, he was accompanied by six muscular attendants.

As the gurney bumped on to the elevator, Mt. Rushmore squeezed Ballantine's arm. "Why you being so negative?" he hissed. "You know the plan."

That's why he was being so negative. Before things got rolling he wondered if he might get scared, but he wasn't scared in the least, just nervous. There was a time when not being scared would have surprised him. When he looked back on it, he realized there hadn't been a day when he hadn't been scared about something or other. That was before his wife got scared to death. After that, nothing scared him.

It wasn't that he no longer gave a shit. He gave a shit. That's why there was nothing they could do to him that was worse than kicking him out. What could they do? Hurt him? Torture him? If they did, it wouldn't work. He was beyond pain. If something hurt too much, he'd up and die. Fuck 'em.

Had he been a reflective man, it might have occurred to Ballantine that being beyond pain gave him a power that approached the superhuman. Maybe this was what Dixon sensed about him. As things stood, though, it had never occurred to him, so he never tested the proposition. None of the executive committee's work required superhuman powers. All it required was the experience and skills each member brought to it. Forty-five years in wholesale fruits and vegetables seemed about as far from the committee's work as it was possible to get, but his experience of going from being scared all the time to not being scared of anything was, as things turned out, extremely useful. More than anything else, it was what permitted the executive committee to do its work.

Until now, Dixon had never been able to get the goods on him. Now she didn't have to. He had punched his own ticket by catching a cold. Any attendant who screwed up this hospital shipment would be an ex-attendant by the end of the day.

As the elevator descended, Mt. Rushmore prattled through a list of all the possible diseases Ballantine might catch in the hospital. "Meningitis, laryngitis, gingivitis, gingitosis, phryngitosis, halitosis, psychosis, thrombosis—"

The prattling irritated Ballantine. "There's no such thing," he snapped.

"As what?"

"Phryngi-fuckin'-whatever."

"You could be the first to get it. Make medical history. Probably name it after you. Like Alzheimer's disease. Schizophrenia. Bunions. Clap."

When he'd interrupted Mt. Rushmore, Ballantine also interrupted the review he'd been conducting of what was to happen the instant they reached the Concourse. They had gone over it and over it. Ballantine grilled every participant on his or her role in a way he would have been embarrassed to do in preparing for a standard executive operation. When they gave him grief about this, he wasn't even slightly embarrassed. This operation was different. His ass was on the line.

John Dillinger was indignant. "Please! We're professionals."

"Well, not exactly," said Mt. Rushmore.

"He knows what I mean," sniffed John Dillinger.

Ballantine didn't hear what she said. He had been pre-occupied with what was to happen the instant the doors opened.

They opened on to the Concourse with, over there, the reception desk, and behind it the waiting area filled with simulated leather-covered loveseats outside the administrative offices. On the other side were the floor-to-ceiling double doors to the dining room. Straight ahead was the main entrance, bevelled glass windows on both sides. A sharp left from the elevator and you were in a corridor as wide as a street that ran past the chapels and the social workers' and financial counsellors' offices, all the way down to the loading dock and the hearses with their motors running, where the ambulance would be pulling up to collect Ballantine and deliver him to the hospital.

Mt. Rushmore said the overall effect reminded him of duty-free areas in old-fashioned airports, but without the shops. And just about everybody who entered the concourse for the first time got the impression that, no matter what it looked like, whatever was going on in it was going on under water, like some aquatic ballet. Everything seemed to move at about one-third normal speed. Even the aides pushing guests toward the front door or into one of the sunrooms that opened off either side of it seemed to move by drifting, or however it was seahorses did. Ballantine always took a deep breath before venturing into the Concourse, as if it would be his last chance to breathe until he made it to wherever he was headed and broke the surface again. Sometimes he'd move his arms as he crossed, doing a breaststroke.

It was a gentle scene, bright with flowery patterns and the soft textures of blankets over knees, that was only prevented from taking on the sweetness of a greeting card by the smell—faint, always more in the back of the throat than the nostrils—of shit and mashed carrots. It was a suspicion of a smell more than a smell, but everybody had exactly the same suspicion, sometimes more shit than mashed carrots, sometimes more mashed carrots than shit. It was how people being admitted as guests knew they weren't dreaming. In dreams there is never any smell.

Ballantine was prepared to see a big crowd of guests waiting for the elevators. As he was pushed through the crowd toward the corridor leading to the back of the building, two women, Chardonnay and Sister Bernice, would come shuffling along in their flip-floppy slippers. Chardonnay would trip. Jesus! Be careful! She'd pitch forward and Sister Bernice would reach out clumsily to keep her from falling, but they'd get messed up together and go down across the gurney's path. Two of Ballantine's attendants would run ahead to untangle them. The others would clear a space through the crowd so the rattled and disoriented old women could be led to seats where they would be safe. The instant their backs were turned, Mt. Rushmore would spin the gurney toward the front entrance. Jimmy McDrool and Banana would hobble out of the crowd to push with him. As more guests flooded into the Concourse from staging areas in the sunrooms, it would be impossible for the attendants to see what had become of their old man.

Out the emergency exit beside the front door. Down the curved drive. Along the sidewalk. Around a corner. And gone.

A straight, no-nonsense escape.

Ballantine would be taken to a safe house until a new identity could be purchased on the Internet and fake documentation prepared by the forgery and digital printing section, which would also cook up some photo I.D. Then he'd be inserted into a fresh consignment of guests being admitted. It was all kind of cumbersome and could take a long time. No one had any idea how long. Maybe months.

four

"MONTHS?!"

It was the first time anybody on the executive committee had heard anything like dismay in Ballantine's voice.
Nobody attending the clandestine meeting in his room,
where security had locked him after tracking him down,
knew what to say. It was the best plan they had been able
to come up with on such short notice. And Ballantine was
part of the planning team, they reminded him.

Now, as the elevator began its descent, he was running
through the plan for probably the hundredth time. Only
this time there was nothing to do but wait for it to play
itself out. What was that noise? A bell ringing somewhere. Bell? Ringing? Telephone? Hey! Mt. Rushmore
wasn't on his cellphone! Why wasn't he alerting
Chardonnay and Sister Bernice that the gurney was on
its way down? Ballantine held his hand to his ear in a
conspicuous signal.

Mt. Rushmore shook his head as inconspicuously as
possible. "Communications glitch," he whispered.

"Communications glitch?!"

"Shhh! I had the phone in my shirt pocket. I took a
leak. When I leaned over to flush, it fell in the toilet."

"In the toilet?!"

Mt. Rushmore nodded sadly.

"Hit the stop button!" Ballantine's whisper was
approaching the guttural. "Go back to my room and get

mine!" The bell ringing in the background was becoming more insistent.

Mt. Rushmore was waggling his hands: Keep it down, keep it down. "In the first place, it *was* yours. The battery in mine died. I tried to dry it out, but there wasn't enough time. And in the second place, I don't have to hit the stop button. We *are* stopped. You didn't notice?"

The fire alarm had triggered the emergency circuits. The elevator had come to a halt between floors.

"What the fuck?"

"Exactly," said Mt. Rushmore. "What the fuck?"

"What do you mean 'What the fuck?'" The bell was becoming louder. "You don't know what the fuck?"

"If I knew what the fuck, why would I say 'What the fuck?'" Mt. Rushmore squeezed his eyes shut in thought. "What do you figure, a fire drill or a gaga?"

"You telling me you didn't assign somebody to set it off?"

"You were at the meeting. You hear anybody assigned to set the fire alarm off?"

"Maybe it was some last-minute wrinkle you decided to throw in."

"When I throw in a fucking—"

One of the attendants was on the elevator phone. "False alarm or something," he told the others, then stuck a key in the control panel. The elevator made a noise like teeth grinding, but it ground on down until it reached the Concourse. The doors opened to clanging so loud that Mt. Rushmore ducked reflexively. Outside was a madhouse, heavy with rising panic, wild, unscripted.

Chardonnay and Sister Bernice were nowhere to be

seen. The attendants escorting Ballantine had to muscle the gurney forward. A nurse's aide grabbed Mt. Rushmore and dragged him to one of the lines headed for a fire exit. Ballantine's attendants plowed through the heaving swarm and out the front entrance to the holding area for least-mobile guests.

Ballantine was mortally depressed. Not even Dixon would risk a snap fire drill, one that was truly spur-of-the-moment. Somebody could get killed. Advance notice always went to nursing stations and chief attendants, and the executive committee's scanner always picked it up— who was to say when it might be worth a great deal to know when there was bound to be chaos? So it must have been a gaga. Guests who were gaga pulled the fire alarm two or three times a week. No one had been able to figure out why, although Ballantine and Mt. Rushmore speculated that it was because they liked the jostling that went with being rounded up and prodded down the stairs. Gagas seemed to enjoy being crammed together and jiggled around. They got pleasure out of it that was incomprehensible to any of the guests who were still able to look after themselves and to communicate and who liked to keep whatever distance they could manage. Sometimes it turned out to be the closest thing to privacy they could hope for. The gagas were highly regarded as neighbours by the committee because they were unexpectedly volatile, making them valuable whenever an irrational diversion was called for.

"The gagas got me."

There was probably a bitter irony in that somewhere, but Ballantine was in no mood to look for it. As soon as the false alarm got sorted out, he was dead. The committee's preparations for his escape were beyond repair. The plan had been cumbersome all right, but worse than that, it had been far too elaborate. The more elaborate things got, the more things could go wrong. When he'd said this at the clandestine committee meeting, everybody said it was about the ten-thousandth time he'd warned them about this. And everybody assured him that it wasn't even half as elaborate as some of the things Ballantine had gone to great pains to keep from becoming too elaborate. He pointed out that this operation was quite a bit different from those. For one thing, nobody was supposed to end up dying in the traditional sense of the word.

He lay back and closed his eyes. He thought about shitting himself just to irritate the ambulance attendants who would soon be driving him away, and to piss off the admitting nurses at the hospital who would already be irritated about getting stuck with some old fart with nothing more serious than a cold.

Better still, if he shit himself he'd be able to feel even sorrier for himself. But he couldn't work anything up.

"Sorry. Just leaning on your rig for a minute."

Ballantine kept his eyes closed. What did he care?

"Quite the show!"

He didn't recognize the voice. Not the voice itself—he wouldn't have been able to identify the voices of more than ten or fifteen guests, but the voice of every guest in The Cloister soon came to have an unmistakable tone: They were busy people. They had things to do. They might not always be certain the things they had to do would get done or would work out the way they intended. But they were getting at them anyway, and any interruption—it was why false alarms quickly lost their charm for anybody who wasn't gaga—had better be able to justify itself.

There was none of the bullshit heartiness that had once infected guests' lives. The Cloister wasn't a service club. Nobody said "Quite the show!" unless they said it derisively. But more than that, the voices of The Cloister weren't uneasy. Only one sort of person would sound anxious about something as inconsequential as leaning on a gurney.

Ballantine opened his eyes. He found himself gazing at an intensely grey man intensely watching the firefighters rush here and there, spreading confusion with their confident aplomb.

"Look at the hose that one has," shrieked one of the knitting ladies.

"It's a big one," shrieked another.

"If I was on fire he wouldn't need a ladder to climb up me," shrieked a third.

"Come over here, honey," cackled the first. "Let me feel how sharp your axe is!"

The intensely grey man was trying to take everything in. He looked as if he was about to hyperventilate.

"What?" he said, turning to look at Ballantine.

"Nothing," said Ballantine, who hadn't said anything. "What?"

"Feel free." Ballantine nodded agreeably.

There were five or six of them—the morning consignment. They looked extremely uncertain, as if they had no idea what they wanted, but were quickly coming to the conclusion that it wasn't this. The grey man stared at him blankly, as if Ballantine had spoken in a language he'd never heard before.

"To lean." Ballantine's hands made make-yourself-at-home circles.

"Oh! Thanks!"

"You didn't get checked in?"

"No! We were in the admitting line when the bell started going."

Ballantine hiked himself up on one elbow. He studied the man carefully. "Got all your stuff there?"

"I don't know where my suitcase and clothes are, but yeah." He held up a folder. Ballantine held out his hand for it and the man passed it to him, then pulled it back quickly. His whole existence was in that folder. But Ballantine kept his hand out, and after a moment the man gave it to him. Ballantine flipped it open.

"Finton."

"Yes!" For some reason, the sound of his own name made the man smile.

"D.K."

"D. *Keith*! You been here awhile?"

"Couple of years." Ballantine was leafing through the documents.

"You like it?" There was an agonizing hope in the question. The rest of the morning consignment stopped watching the firefighters and leaned in to hear what Ballantine would say.

"It's okay. Been able to get lots done."

They looked mystified. The grey man said, "You still in business or something?"

Ballantine closed his eyes and let his chin sink to his

chest. D. *Keith* Finton, he thought. Good old D. *Keith*. I don't owe you anything.

"You've still got the rest of your life ahead of you."

"I'm sorry?"

Shit. Talk about embarrassing. He'd said that right out loud. He was going to have to improvise.

"I mean, you've got some of the best parts of your life still to live."

If he was going to improvise, he might as well do it shamelessly. D. Keith would recognize the cordiality from years past, when things were certain and truths came from the heart. It would have the ring of fellowship to him, and fellowship was something he'd have spent his life seeking and, once found, dispensing in return. He would take it as an encouraging expression of generous and immediate acceptance, a veteran extending his strong, welcoming hand to a greenhorn.

He would be moved even more deeply when his new friend said, "Bet you haven't slept much the last couple of nights. How about I get down off here and you can get up and rest? Spell each other off."

"But—but—"

Ballantine was smiling for the first time in days. "All I got is a little cold. They don't like chances around here. First sign of a cold, they give you a ride everywhere. Treat you like royalty."

"Are you sure?" D. Keith's eyes got even more watery than they had been.

"Of course." He slid to the ground. "Here, let me give you a hand getting up."

Then, clutching D. Keith's file like it was diamonds, Ballantine evaporated into the crowd.

five

THE MINUTE HE HAD STARTED to sniffle, Ballantine's name was scrubbed from the next scheduled execution and London Derriere, who thought it would be good to get out and see how things worked in the field, volunteered to fill in. Somebody was always happy to lend a hand. There weren't so many executions that everybody got a chance to be involved much beyond the committee stage. London Derriere had been most closely associated with the executive committee's community outreach program and this was her chance to take part in what she described as "the pointy end" of the work.

As a result, instead of blowing the living shit right out of the chairman of Big One Confederated Bank on the fourteenth hole of the Rosewell Golf Club, Ballantine got a chance to sleep in. It was a start toward recuperating from three days on the run, getting captured, devising a plan to keep from getting sent to hospital, then seeing it unravel, and then having to pull something out of a hat at the last minute. He looked over at the pictures of what he assumed were D. Keith Finton's family, which he had arranged on the top of the dresser after unpacking D. Keith's stuff. The fact that he was lying there wondering who these people were meant his desperation move had worked. It was beyond him how anybody, even if they weren't all that bright, could mistake the guest they had to strap down on the gurney in the holding pen for the nearly catatonic one they had left there twenty minutes earlier. Wouldn't they have paid some attention to his horrified blithering about not even having checked in yet, so why were they forcing him into an ambulance? Ballantine and D. Keith didn't look even vaguely alike and Ballantine had been fatalistically still from the moment he was rolled off the elevator. Did they even notice the change in behaviour? Or if they did, did they simply assume that the guest had gone violently gaga since the fire alarm started ringing? Stranger things had happened.

One of the strangest happened a few minutes after that when Ballantine, who had been living in The Cloister for two years and was Number One on Dixon's Troublemakers List, reached the front of the line at the reception desk, handed over D. Keith Finton's file, signed himself in as a new guest with an obvious forgery, and nobody so much as blinked. He kept waiting for Dixon to send somebody to grab him by the neck and kick him out the front door. But nothing happened, not even when the attendant who showed up to take him to his new room turned out to be one of the six who had carted him out of his old room that morning. Ballantine wondered if he would end up in his old room, which he would have liked because he'd gotten used to coming and going from there and it would have made it easier for his daughters to find him on their next visit, but his new address was one floor up and on the other side of the building. He didn't much care, though. One room was exactly like every other, and a change was as good as a rest.

Ballantine was being less than completely honest when he told Mt. Rushmore that his first impulse when he woke up as D. Keith Finton was to rush downstairs and say there had been a terrible mistake and get himself sent off to the hospital and D. Keith installed in his rightful place.

That was okay, because Mt. Rushmore didn't believe him for one minute. "Bullshit," he said.

"It's like I was preying on a helpless old person. I'm supposed to be a sworn defender of old people. Somebody who fights for them and—"

"Bullshit."

"—is willing to—why do you keep saying 'Bullshit'?"

"Because it's bullshit. Nobody ever said anything about defending old people. The only thing that has to do with old people is that you are one. And me. And the others. But that's just circumstances. We happen to be here. And the only important thing now that you're back is that we can get back to work. And the numbers are right."

He was definitely right about how important it was that the numbers were right. Ballantine had been thinking about that while he lay in bed recovering from his cold the first morning of his new life as a Finton. Just as a guest too few got Dixon rampaging around because maximum capacity was always to be maintained, a guest too many ate into the profits. Some disparity had tipped Dixon off that a guest was on the run—a reduction in toilet paper use in a guest room (because Ballantine had gone into hiding), without a corresponding decrease in food consumption (because the executive committee were sneaking portions out of the dining room for him). So it was only a matter of time before they found Ballantine behind the bulletproof vests and plexiglass shields in the security locker where the riot gear was stowed. Not that Dixon was surprised to discover the culprit was Ballantine, but there would have been hell to pay no matter who it was.

The thing that bothered him most about what Mt. Rushmore said was the idea that if he'd disappeared from The Cloister, the executions would have stopped. It wasn't them stopping that concerned him. He didn't care about that one way or the other. What concerned him was the idea that what was going on was going on because he was there. He didn't like the implication, which appeared to be the same one Dixon had grasped: That his presence explained something or other. It certainly didn't explain everything.

six

WHAT WITH ONE THING and another, Ballantine wouldn't have minded not slipping out of The Cloister at 5:30 a.m. and jumping on the subway, then transferring to a city bus and then another that would leave him and the rest of the crew with a twenty-minute walk to where their gear was buried in the woods behind the fourteenth tee of the Rosewell Golf Club.

"There is minimum security," Sister Bernice said at the final briefing. "Just this fence." She tapped the map with her pointer. The pointer, the map stuck to the wall with masking tape, and the flip chart Sister Bernice used for briefings gave Speed the screaming meemies.

"We could do PowerPoint," he kept reminding her. "We could animate. Play it out in real time. I could get you a laser pointer. We—"

"I'm an old lady," was all she'd say. "Even a flip chart confuses me."

"Aw, for—"

"Now, while I say this fence represents minimum security, the actual security at Rosewell Golf Club is maximum if you count exclusivity, prestige, social position, and the cost of membership, which is extreme, but does not figure into the decision anyone considered a suitable member makes when they join."

"Is this a briefing or a commentary on Western society?" Mt. Rushmore whispered.

Ballantine shook his head. "I don't know," he said. "I never played golf."

"Let me put it to you this way," Sister Bernice went on. "To stand on the fourteenth tee of Rosewell is to be protected by the legions of history and privilege. Not—it goes without saying—that bank chairmen usually have that much family history. It still is"—she sounded as if she was reminding her listeners that it wasn't too late, that there were career opportunities they might consider—"it still is entirely possible to rise from the teller's wicket to the office with the commanding view and the genuine oil paintings. But once you get there—"

"How come you never got there, Sister Bernice?"

The shot came from John Dillinger, who never missed a chance to take a shot at other women for not having what it takes.

"I was overqualified," Sister Bernice shot back. "Now"—whapping the map with her pointer—"even a bank chairman, once he's in, is granted full entitlement. Because, by getting to the top of the heap, he'll have learned what everyone who was born there just naturally knows is the most important thing of all. And that's the position of everybody else."

"You should stay awake." Mt. Rushmore nudged Ballantine. "There's no telling what you might learn."

Ballantine snerfled. He always fell asleep during Sister Bernice's briefings.

"The chairman of a bank," she concluded gravely, "is respected because he shows respect, and anybody who controls that much money and will kiss your ass deserves a membership in your golf club."

"From what I can make of it," Mt. Rushmore said, and got up and peered at the map closely, "if you miss the fourteenth fairway, you'll probably feel like killing yourself."

The executive team's approach had been scouted, measured, timed, memorized, rehearsed. The tactical devices, which had drawn enormous praise for Jimmy McDrool, had gone into the ground two nights earlier. The explosive components had been acquired by Fastrack and Speed from offshore suppliers who were happy to accept the Euros that Fastrack was happy to get rid of because he wasn't sure they were as clean as they ought to be. The detonation system had been converted from a remote-control garage door opener. McDrool rebuilt it in the basement workshop where guests were offered occupational-therapy lectures paid for by the government and taught by a craftsman who was so confident in his knowledge and training skills that it never occurred to him that the course he gave, one session for each of the seventeen stages of home renovation, was of no use to these students and of no interest either. Yet the classes were overbooked and the attention the participants paid, especially to esoteric techniques, was intense. Questions were invariably detailed and probing, and the guests were always coming up with the damnedest projects. That was why there were so many complex precision tools and machines, although this stuff had nothing on the electronic stuff next door in what the guests referred to as Muppet Labs. Fortunately, there was always some kind of government grant available to pay for anything they needed, or a church group keen to raise money, or a company willing to make a donation so its chief executive officer could have his beaming picture taken, surrounded by nittering old goofs, beside his generously provided micron fignofanomometer, or whatever the committee had set the scroungers to acquiring. It knocked the guests out to see these presentation photographs in the neighbourhood weekly, and they practised appropriate expressions until they pissed their pants laughing. The "just-had-a-lobotomy, but-doing-fine" smile was Sister Bernice's specialty. Of course Jimmy McDrool had no trouble coming up with a trickle down the side of his chin that caught the light appealingly. Since the stroke, he had one all the time.

Sometimes when he'd had a few drinks from the still in Skunk Hollow, the carefully concealed supply room behind Muppet Labs, Speed would talk with wonder about how close The Cloister was to having nuclear capability, and would urge Ballantine to have the initiatives subcommittee examine the possibility of whether certain countries, or at least their capital cities, couldn't usefully be executed the same as individuals were. This always made Mt. Rushmore paranoid. Once you start moving beyond deserving individuals, you risked retaliation, escalation—not that anyone would know whom to retaliate against, but that wouldn't matter. In international situations, when it became strategically necessary to have enemies, it didn't make any difference who they were. The possibility of creating a rapidly spreading world disorder made him urge that their work be restricted to the originally agreed-upon limits: Only targets that could be reached by public transit.

The chairman of Big One Confederated Bank was up a hundred and seventy-five dollars after thirteen holes and was at the top of his backswing on the fourteenth tee when the living shit was blown right out of him. The noise made by the focused charges wasn't all that loud, just as McDrool had promised, given the open surroundings. A dry crack. The chairman's playing partners thought he must have been struck by lightning. The turf was charred where he'd taken his stance. They looked heavenward and, true to their best judgment and long years on the golf course, and despite the sun being bright and the sky clear blue, ran and stood under the tallest nearby tree. They stood there for some minutes, wondering what to do about the fallen chairman, and whether it was safe to venture out to check. When they did, they were sickened. It was the first time any of them had seen anyone with the living shit blown out of him. Already players from following foursomes were crowding around the tee; some of the gagging sounds were louder than the explosion had been. Golfers lining up putts on the thirteenth green craned to see what was causing the delay ahead of them. Soon there were half a dozen riding carts and four or five pullcarts on the asphalt path beside the tee. Gingerly, one or two golfers approached the chairman, then hesitated. What if lightning struck twice? Somebody suggested phoning for help, and a dozen cellphones were pulled out of a dozen golf bags. A dozen callers called 911. A senior member volunteered to go ahead to the clubhouse and seek assistance from there. There were jokes about him just wanting to play through, but he said he'd borrow somebody's cart and be right back. Another senior member volunteered to ride along as backup, then a woman who complained of chest pains brought on by all the excitement, squeezed on board and they buzzed away.

By the time they reached the clubhouse, a fire truck was already screaming into the parking lot and firefighters with respirators and first-aid kits started asking everybody where the victim was. The senior members in the golf cart pulled alongside and tried to give directions, but it was difficult with everybody shouting. Two police cars swooped in, then an ambulance that followed the fire truck up the middle of the eighteenth fairway, lights flashing, firefighters whooping and holding on gallantly as it crested rises. Then another ambulance appeared and one of the senior members in the golf cart—but not, as the crowd back at the fourteenth tee would have assumed, the woman who complained about chest pains—clutched his chest and fell to the ground and the ambulance would have run over him if the other senior members hadn't waved frantically to halt it. They pleaded to have the gasping old fellow taken to a hospital, something the paramedics felt obliged by the code of the mobile medevac services to do even though they were clearly unhappy about passing up a chance to get a first-hand look at somebody who'd had the living shit blown right out of him by lightning. They strapped the old man on a stretcher while his pals, clambering aboard and hanging on for dear life, told their friend to hang in there as they swayed viciously through traffic toward the nearest emergency department.

"We were going to just wander off to a bus stop, as per the original plan," London Derriere reported during the debriefing, "but when Jorgy saw the ambulance, he said 'Hey, stick with me' and collapsed. It was the best seizure I've ever seen."

Jorgy blushed and said he'd tried to remember how he'd behaved the time he'd had a real one, and thrown in a couple of bits of business he'd picked up from watching guests around The Cloister pop off.

Jimmy McDrool was pleased to hear how well the focused charges had worked. He had modified very small, very powerful landmines that Speed and Fastrack ordered through a Czech dealer they'd found trolling for customers in an Internet arms-trade chat room. The entire tee area had been so carefully sown with them that no matter where the greenskeepers set the tees that morning, the feet of the chairman of Big One Confederated were bound to be near three or four, which would be set off using selected frequencies and do the job without endangering his fellow players.

At the emergency department, while the paramedics were arguing with the nurses who didn't want a geriatric cardiac case, London Derriere and Harry the Hat unbuckled the straps and helped Jorgy off the stretcher. They walked through a pair of doors and, after one or two false leads, found themselves in a hallway that led to the hospital's main entrance. Though Jorgy offered to buy a round of decaf, skim-milk lattes at the Starbucks in the hospital lobby, London Derriere and Harry the Hat said they'd buy him one, but at the other end, at the outlet beside the subway stop up the street from The

Cloister. So they hustled, as much as they ever did, or as much as they could, on their way.

No one involved in planning and carrying out the execution had considered the possibility that it might be mistaken for lightning. They just expected that an explosion that killed the chairman of the biggest bank in the country on the back nine of the most exclusive golf club in the country would be startling enough to confuse everyone. It never occurred to them that for three days, until the yellow police tape was taken down and the greenskeepers were allowed to dig up the fourteenth tee to prepare the ground for its reconstruction and the remaining wicked-looking little explosive charges, neatly arranged from one end to the other, were discovered, the chairman's death would be listed by the authorities as an act of God.

seven

JORGY DIED THAT NIGHT and, after the service to wish him goodbye, Mt. Rushmore came up to Ballantine and said it was a pity that on the very day he became famous for pretending to have such a spectacular seizure in the parking lot of the Rosewell Golf Club, nobody was around to appreciate the real seizure he had before he was found in the elevator after leaving the Evening Cookie Club early, apologizing for being so tired he couldn't keep his eyes open. He was in no shape to enjoy his second ride in an ambulance that day and was D.O.A. at the hospital. This made him extremely popular with the ambulance crew because they didn't have to fight with the nurses about dropping him off, and extremely popular with the nurses because they didn't have to admit him.

Whenever something like this happened to someone who had been energetically involved in the work of the executive committee, which it did with remarkable frequency, Ballantine wondered how long people would be interested in keeping the work going. Sometimes he wondered if there were even enough guests who could follow exactly what it was the committee was doing, much less take part. A lot of the time he wasn't sure he could, but when he faltered, he found falling back on the will of the majority a great and often seductive help. When he'd murdered Asshole No. 2, Ballantine had been both the majority and the minority—all he'd had to fall back on was his own reedy will and the enormous amount of information he'd had to acquire. "Calculating a trajectory requires a grasp of quadratic equations, physics, geometry, and meteorology and is one of the reasons members of the artillery fairly consider themselves a cut or two above the scum who fill the other branches of the armed services," he read in a textbook he'd found in a secondhand bookstore devoted to military matters. But Ballantine had always been proficient with numbers. Keeping track of large quantities of perishables over varying distances and periods of time, and knowing how much you could get away with charging for them if there had been hitches along the way, was central to the wholesale fruits and vegetables business. As far as he could recall, the only important thing was always to put the fresh on top.

Soon he was familiar enough with the variables to be confident that he could launch Asshole No. 2 from the waist-high retaining wall beside the dumpsters in the low-income apartment development, up and over a crabapple tree that had somehow survived thirty years of social housing and poverty landscaping, and into the tennis court that had been wired shut from the day it was built and protected from tennis players by coils of razor wire around the top of the fence that enclosed it. Compared to a shot at the buzzer from the other end of the floor in a basketball game, the tennis court was a big target and Asshole No. 2 a small projectile. And the possibility of the shot falling short and striking someone in the ratty area between the launch site and the target area was zero, since it was a gang-established demilitarized zone. Anyone who wandered into it after midnight when

Ballantine intended to slam-dunk Asshole No. 2 was going to wind up dead anyway, and knew it.

At the time, Ballantine didn't think this was particularly complicated. As far as he was concerned, it was what was necessary, although later on he would never have approved a scheme anywhere near as elaborate. He had to concentrate really hard to keep track of all the strands, and this was helpful because if he wasn't paying close attention to something specific, he tended not to pay attention to anything. Great chunks of time simply disappeared. Figuring out how to kill Asshole No. 2 kept him involved in his own life. He made a great many diagrams and searched a great many catalogues to find everything he needed. It was from a yachting supplier that he procured the heavy steel cleat he would bolt to the masonry palisade on the roof of Asshole No. 2's building, directly above the wall where he sat to receive the money from his four younger sisters and to direct their energies as the night wore on. The key to the whole project was the most basic of all psychological responses: Unless you were a psychopath, the sudden appearance of a police officer who spoke and behaved in a tough and authoritative manner caused you to do exactly what the officer said to do. This, which Ballantine and the committee would later refine brilliantly when dealing with Mr. and Mrs. Merrick, the real-estate moguls, was especially the case among people accustomed to police officers appearing suddenly and ordering them around. The less they dicked around, the sooner they were back on the street conducting business. So if the officer shouted "Freeze, asshole," you froze. If the officer said, "Assume the position, asshole," you leaned forward with your hands against the wall or the roof of the car and waited patiently to be frisked.

When Ballantine materialized out of the darkness, identified himself as a detective, and told Asshole No. 2 to put his hands behind his back, there was no doubt in his mind that Asshole No. 2 would obligingly prepare himself to be handcuffed. Ballantine could slip the chain linking the cuffs through a loop in the bungee cord. He would kick loose the anchor holding the bungee cord taut, firing Asshole No. 2 upward. Having reached the limits of its elasticity, the cord would pull itself free of the vertically mounted cleat Ballantine had bolted to the rooftop parapet. And, finally, Asshole No. 2 would sail high over the crabapple tree before smashing against the asphalt of the tennis court with sufficient force that even if he didn't happen to land on his head, it would kill him.

Ballantine lived every second of the preview, working out each detail, recalculating each angle. The amount of bungee cord that would be required weighed nearly as much as Ballantine did, which was far heavier than anything he could move for more than a very short distance. It took him five whole nights just to heave it up the seven flights of fire stairs and on to the roof. The only complication had been the drug addicts who complained that he was disrupting their meditations as he dragged the bundle past. The night he finally got to the top with it, he was amazed to discover he had the roof to himself and, although by the time he dragged it to the base of the parapet he was so weary his limbs were trembling and he was about to vomit, he wanted to make sure he could at least hoist the bundle to the parapet ledge. This, he would later realize, was unnecessary. When the time came for final preparations, he could feed the bungee cord over like a long snake. Exertion had clouded his thinking. And, as he struggled to hoist it the last fraction of a bit, his last puff of strength seeped away. And along with his strength went the last iota of control—he could hear blood vessels bursting in his temples. Instead of balancing on the parapet, the heavy mass of bungee cord pitched forward under its own momentum and rolled off into space. In the instant before Ballantine blacked out, he saw it plunge downward and strike Asshole No. 2 square on the top of the head. It wasn't until after he regained consciousness and was steady enough to climb down the stairs that he made his way past the crowd at the ambulance and heard someone say something about a "neckbone snapped clean in two."

He wasn't sure whether he'd grown tired of telling this story or whether the people he told it to kept dying off and he'd grown tired of that. Taking people into your confidence at The Cloister was risky. Confiding in someone required trust, and after awhile, you got tired of establishing trust when the person you established it with was liable to conk out before you saw him again, which you had expected to do an hour later at beanbag class. Not that Ballantine boasted—quite the opposite. As often as not, a newcomer would pick up a version of the story that had got a little rearranged, a little overblown, as it drifted up and down the corridors and through the sunrooms where it floated in ever more mindless circles. That was how the sharpened steel stake had replaced Ballantine as the lethal arrow in the legendary retelling of Asshole No. 1's murder.

And how the anvil came to smash Asshole No. 2's brains out and then—yanked back by the recoiling bungee cord and hauled in over the edge of the roof by Ballantine—was never discovered as the murder weapon. If only the anvil could have disappeared during its return journey to the roof, it would have been a perfect crime: The vanishing murder weapon. Although, hell, it was a perfect crime anyway. Ballantine felt duty bound to correct these misconceptions—"I wouldn't even know where to shop for an anvil"—and as a result found himself retelling his story, even though everyone just thought he was being far too modest. Besides, given the choice, it was something he'd rather talk about than his daughters.

Nevertheless, in whatever form it got passed around the building, often turning up in even-more spectacular versions, it did a great deal to confirm his reputation as a first-class serial killer, a man who could get the job done, time after time. It was the inspirational presence of such a man among them that gave the guests at The Cloister hope and courage, and clear evidence that if there was a thing or two they wanted to set straight, it could be done, and they could do it. The result was as profound as it would have been if the air in the building had been replaced with helium and the guests had all filled up like balloons and floated around above the floor.

Something like that doesn't go unnoticed by a management for whom the most subdued guest is the most cost-efficient. It didn't take long to home in on the exact moment the disturbing change occurred, or for Ballantine's records to be removed from the general files and placed in a locked drawer in Dixon's desk.

e i g h t

BALLANTINE'S REFUSAL TO SEE himself as anything more than a bit player who turned up by chance was why he didn't jump out of his skin at lunchtime when the lady who smelled like V8 juice, who had arrived in the morning contingent, piped up. The first thing she did was ask if anybody had ever murdered anybody. Murder had become such a standard topic among The Cloister's guests that Ballantine forgot it wasn't a question that a new arrival might be expected to ask, and, by way of making neighbourly conversation, told her that he, personally, had had considerable success with bungee cord. But all she did was say she had no idea what he was talking about. Maybe she had forgotten what bungee cord was. And what Ballantine said wasn't strictly accurate—it was more a subjective opinion than objective truth. Bungee cord wasn't listed as a factor in the official records of the three deaths that constituted his solo career. But then, invisibility wasn't listed as a factor either. Invisibility was a factor that not even Ballantine had factored in.

The lady said it was an abusive husband. Not hers. Not any more. This time around it was her granddaughter's.

"Jesus Christ!" said Mt. Rushmore, taking off his glasses and stirring them around in the green Jell-O on his tray.

The lady's V8 smell couldn't be smelled across the table. Ballantine noticed it when the social-interaction therapist led her around to each guest seated at the table

61

and introduced her. He didn't catch her name. She watched Mt. Rushmore stir his Jell-O for a minute, then said, "There's a court order. But there's been court orders before. There's always a court order somewhere or other."

"Jesus Christ!" Mt. Rushmore plunged his glasses into his cup of tea. He glared at the Jell-O. "I thought that was my tea!"

Her father had been abusive, her husband had been abusive, her daughter's husband had been abusive. Now it was her granddaughter's husband.

"Genetic!" Mt. Rushmore wiped his glasses on his shirt.

"I don't want this one to get away with it."

"Nothing anybody here can do about something like that," Mt. Rushmore said.

There was no rule as such, but it was generally agreed that the dining-room table wasn't the best place to talk about personal problems, not because no one was interested, but because if one guest aired them out, then everybody else felt entitled to do the same and things could drag on and on and nobody would get anything done. Sometimes new guests took awhile to catch on. The lady folded her hands on the edge of the table and stared at them for a long time. Finally, without looking up, she said, "I have something."

"Me, too! Diabetes!" Mrs. Don't Touch Hutch sensed an opening and her voice was full of the sympathy and one-upmanship that was central to social conversations in The Cloister. "Bad ticker, too!" She pointed to her chest. "Had a stroke!" She rapped her knuckles on her skull. "This arm's not worth shit!" With her left hand she raised her right arm above her head and let go. It dropped into her lap with a thump. "If somebody cuts my food, it's all right." Clearly she began to feel uncomfortable about hogging the limelight, so, pointing at Mt. Rushmore, she said, "He had a colostomy! Wears a bag!" Mt. Rushmore's eyes snapped wide. Even after a few years, it was still surprising how out loud everybody lived, and not just their own lives.

"Jimmy McDrool"—she appeared to be ready to go all the way around the table, but that was as far as she got because the newcomer was paying no attention and carried right on with what she'd been saying.

"I have a gun," she said.

"Jesus Christ!"

"A Glock nine-millimetre automatic. The police came when I fell, and I slipped it out of one of the young women's holsters." Somehow she had managed to keep it hidden in the hospital and during months of convalescence. "Upstairs." She pointed toward the ceiling. "The police officer was with me for a long time before the ambulance came. She never noticed."

Ballantine avoided Mt. Rushmore's smeary stare. They knew where they could get guns, but as far as they knew, this was the first guest to arrive armed.

He avoided looking at the V8 lady. He wondered what he smelled like. Nobody had ever said anything to him. But a lot of people smelled like shit and he never said anything to them.

"Maureen!" a voice roared.

There was a jittery rustle in the dining room. Somebody started screaming. "Shut the fuck up!" the screamer screamed.

"Maureen, it is I!" the voice roared.

"I know who the fuck it is! Fuck off!"

Mt. Rushmore always doubted that Screaming Maureen's late husband ever used the grammatical construction "It is I" when he was alive. Ballantine had never heard of anybody who talked like that. Maybe there was a stipulation that voices from beyond the grave had to talk like voices from beyond the grave. Screaming Maureen wasn't a very robust screamer. Her voice was thin and frail, and sounded like someone screaming while they were being smothered with a pillow. It was enough to get the other screamers going, though, especially the dozen or so gagas who were fed with the other guests. Even the V8 lady who had never heard Screaming Maureen and her late husband go at each other was letting out involuntary yips.

"Maureen!"

The discomfort that filled the room made Ballantine think what it must be like to walk barefoot on thistles. Heavy slams sounded over the screams as the staff rushed out and the dining room doors were closed.

"It is I!"

Voices here and there responded in a chant that was high and wavering. "It is he! It is he!"

"Maureen! Can you hear me?"

"Can you hear him?" Guests' voices shrilled as more joined in. "Can you hear him?"

Everyone felt a powerful compulsion to do something, but no one knew what. Chairs were knocked over as guests tried ponderously to stand. The chairs hit other guests rising on shaky legs. Gnarled figures were sent sprawling under tables, the wind knocked out of them. The thing Ballantine felt he should do was stay put because other times he'd fled for the sides of the room and been brought down by a caroming walker or cracked across the nose by a cane pinwheeling through the air, but Mt. Rushmore lunged past, toppling him sideways. Guests who managed to remain on their feet stumbled among the tables, trying to avoid being dragged down by clawed fingers grabbing at their legs from below.

"Maureen!"

"Maureen! Maureen!" they chanted.

"Maureen!" called Maureen's husband from beyond the grave. "I've been having great sex up here. I've been fucking my brains out!"

The chorus of screams grew so loud it seemed to squeeze Ballantine's ribcage and make it impossible to inhale. Hands got stepped on. Bones snapped. Guests who made it as far as the doors pushed desperately against them, but there was no escape. They were locked from the outside.

"There are lots of women up here. Beautiful women. Young broads with big tits and hot lips who love to fuck and suck. Not like you, you scrawny old cunt."

No amount of screaming could drown it out.

The guests had brought in electricians to examine the public address system and search for a cut-out that some-body could use to make pornographic announcements to humiliate Screaming Maureen, but the lines hadn't been tampered with. Guests who had spent their lives working with complicated electronic equipment wired sensors into the circuitry to detect transmissions from some outside source, but these invariably showed no external input. The more effort put into checking the system, the more evi-dent it became that there was no earthly explanation, and the more guests panicked when the voice taunted Screaming Maureen about sexual triumphs after death.

Two guests were pronounced dead at the scene after this latest outburst, eleven others were taken from the dining room with fractures and internal injuries. One of the ambulance buses the city had purchased in the event of an airliner crashing or a terrorist attack had been called when the screaming started and was waiting outside, its emergency lights pulsing blue through the dining-room windows. The injured guests were dropped at a number of hospitals, where they were piled in the corridors between the emergency departments and the intensive care units. New guests had been moved into their rooms at The Cloister by the end of the day. Capacity was maintained.

What should be done about the new guest with the gun was a question that would have come up at that night's executive committee meeting if it hadn't been postponed so everybody could regain their bearings after the excitement, but The Shadow broke into the V8 lady's room while she was napping and confirmed that she had one all right.

"Glock. Police issue. Very well maintained," she reported. "No ammo, though. Except what's in the clip."

The V8 lady was obviously ready for action, but it didn't sound as if she was prepared to carry it out herself. And she wasn't very discreet. There was no need for a lot of discretion if you knew the ropes, but she had only just moved in. Could it be a coincidence, or had she known the ropes before she arrived? Ballantine wondered about that. If she knew—someone who was, as far as anybody could tell, a stranger to all the other guests—who else did? Who else on the outside?

nine

IT WAS ALWAYS DIFFICULT for Ballantine to remain objective when he judged a candidate. And it wasn't always easy to gauge the emotional states of the other members of the executive committee. Some had no objectivity at all, and went along with the general drift as soon as they caught it for the pleasure of being on the winning side. How wrought up were members who spoke out strongly? Were they being swept along by some crazy passion, or had they reached a considered, level-headed decision that the nominated individual had no business damaging the lives of others, and it was time he or she was stopped for good and always? Did committee members sitting around the table in the crafts room have a personal angle they were hiding? Had they been fucked over and wanted a chance to get even? Was it just something about a particular candidate they couldn't stand—wardrobe, facial tic? It wouldn't have been enough that the chairman of Big One Confederated Bank had arranged the financing that flooded all of Venezuela and resulted in eight and a half million inhabitants of the backwaters who couldn't have got out in time even if they'd been warned, being drowned, and an equal number who managed to get out in time starved. That was business. There is more to a person's life than business. His personal life had to be every bit as disgusting. And despite a powerful case made in defence of the chairman, one of the most extensively and carefully prepared the executive committee ever heard, the vote to off him was seventeen to zero, the chairman's advocate abstaining.

But it had been a tricky and complicated matter, and Ballantine became concerned when things got that way, although blowing the living shit out of the chairman of Big One Confederated Bank with modified Czech land-mines purchased through a numbered offshore account as he reached the top of his backswing on the fourteenth tee of the Rosewell Golf Club was not, by Ballantine's measure, tricky or complicated. No ruse was required to entice the candidate to a certain spot at a certain time. If you don't count the golf attire, it hadn't turned into a costume drama, something even the simplest executions had a way of doing. There was no one-shot immediacy about the execution: If the weather didn't co-operate, if the chairman skipped his regular round, if a replacement field operator hadn't been available when Ballantine came down with a cold, they would have been happy to put it off for a week, two weeks, as long as they wanted. In a way, once an execution was voted through, all the rest was detail. Selecting a potential candidate—the nomination procedures, the hearing, the prosecution, the defence, the deliberations, the vote itself—this was where the hard work got done, the tough choices were made, where the big questions got asked and were satis-factorily answered, or no blood got spilled. And the conclusion Ballantine arrived at after his first solo effort proved again and again to be the essence of success. Careful planning and attention to detail—they pay off.

Fastrack understood intuitively because the people

who planned carefully and paid close attention to detail became so confident they were doing the right thing that they would give him money to blow on lunatic ventures nobody in their right mind ever thought would pay off. To him it was obvious, just as it was obvious to Fastrack that the executive committee should have a boiler room. Guests like Ballantine, who knew he didn't mean the kind where you find the furnace, always asked, "Why?"

"You'll see," Fastrack replied.

The guests who thought he was talking about the kind where you find the furnace said they thought The Cloister already had a boiler room. He said he meant a different kind. "What kind?" they asked. "You'll see," he told them.

He kept saying "You'll see" when he started hanging around, offering Ballantine advice. It disturbed Ballantine when people offered him advice. Why would they give him advice? If they wanted something done, why didn't they take their own advice and do it? If Ballantine wanted advice, he was happy to ask for it, but people didn't give him advice because he asked. They did it because, as far as they were concerned, he was in charge. As far as Ballantine was concerned, nobody was in charge and, if somebody was, it wasn't him. Fastrack didn't buy that. He had never been the kind of person to take "You're out of your fucking mind" for an answer. It was the secret of his success. It also explained why he ended up in The Cloister. It was all he could afford. And he knew one thing for sure—if nobody was in charge, it was Ballantine.

Fastrack was the kind of person who couldn't stand doing nothing but, when he moved into The Cloister, had reached the stage of life where nobody wanted him to do anything any more. There was retired when people said, "So, what are you going to do now that you're retired?" And after that kind of retirement there was The Cloister, where people didn't say anything because once you moved in, it was obvious you were no longer up to doing anything. Your days of doing things were done. This outraged him. But if that's the way people were going to be, fine. He'd show them: He'd never do anything again. That would teach them!

When people made their minds up in such a determined way, they became the kind of marks Fastrack could go to town on, which was how he came to be in a perfect position to take advantage of himself after Ballantine moved in.

"I was in boiler rooms my whole life," he told Ballantine.

"I know," said Ballantine. "You've said so many times."

"Professionally I was in a discount brokerage. Phone sales, cold calls. We never sold anything worth more than two cents, but we always made it sound like it was worth fifty bucks. Then we offered it to the customers for ten. A forty-dollar discount. Who could turn down a deal like that? I did very nicely. But those who much is given to should give something back, so I did a little service in my community."

"Yes," said Ballantine. "I know."

Fastrack had trapped Ballantine during beanbag class. Beanbag class wasn't mandatory, but the relatives of guests who didn't show up received a note from Dixon suggesting that the guests were losing interest in their personal well-being, which could indicate depression, and perhaps psychiatric testing was called for. Since this meant the guests would never be seen again, nobody missed beanbag class, but since there was nothing about tossing a beanbag back and forth that enhanced your interest in your personal well-being, most people just stood around, which made them easy prey for Fastrack, who came to beanbag class for the express purpose of trapping them.

"I set up at my own expense a community-based boiler room, nights and weekends. Through it I was able to offer my friends and neighbours—what we called 'select clientele'—things that were not always available through my regular discount boiler room. Why should they be denied the chance to take advantage of certain investment opportunities just because certain avenues were closed off due to regulatory inconsistencies or a temporary shortness of fiduciary wherewithal? You"—he pointed at Ballantine—"should have something like that working for you. Your business is going to start growing."

"I'm not in business. There is no business." Ballantine scrunched up his face in a genuine effort to get the message through. "If there's business, I don't know about it."

"You'll see." Fastrack would walk away from these conversations whistling tunelessly. Tunelessly is the only way you can whistle when your lips have dried out permanently and the skin is so thin it's transparent. None of the guests in The Cloister could whistle tunefully any more, and they knew it. When somebody whistled, they did it to get on your nerves.

Having by this time murdered nine people, either in cold blood or as an accessory before, during, and after the fact, Ballantine was pleased to discover that some things could still get on his nerves. Before he started knocking people off full-time, he would have assumed that you would gradually grow emotionally armour-plated. It hadn't happened. He took great pleasure in a job well done, and if a job got screwed up, he honestly doubted his capacities and worried that he might not be cut out for the work. Never had he felt anything but profound sadness as he looked at an individual whose life was about to be snuffed out, or failed to think how unfortunate it was that anybody could be so unworthy and unkind a human being as to deserve to get snuffed. He had grown up being told by an industrious mother that there was a little streak of goodness in everybody, no matter how wickedly they treated everybody else, and he'd spent his working life believing that, even though every day in the wholesale fruits and vegetables business he encountered people who, to judge by their dealings with him, were missing that little streak. Now that he realized that he and his mother had been mistaken, he devoted his greatest energy to looking for even a little hint of a streak in every candidate nominated for execution and making sure that no one who got selected had anything whatsoever that anybody even for a moment might consider good. If good was too much to ask for, then, at the very minimum, nice.

It was why Mrs. Marilyn Merrick was in Pastures of Plenty Cemetery and why Mr. Murray Merrick wasn't lying beside her, but merely in a federal penitentiary for putting her there, although he claims he was framed, and certainly was. Theirs had been the first double candidacy submitted to the executive committee.

Mrs. Marilyn and Mr. Murray Merrick had been in the real estate business and visible on far more than billboards as wide as the wingspan of a jumbo jet. They had their own reality show on cable TV, something that was extremely unusual for someone who wasn't a show business legend, even though Mt. Rushmore said pretty soon more people would have cable TV reality shows than there would be people to watch them. This was certainly far from the case in The Cloister, where the only reality show on the in-house cable was Mt. Rushmore's "News & Views Roundup," and the only other show of any kind was the Sunday service from the Big Auditorium where Minimum Max preached unintelligibly to the gagas. Mt. Rushmore wasn't being critical when he mentioned the growing number of cable TV reality shows. He believed everybody should have one, and was gratified by his audience, which, on peak days when there was a lot of reality to contend with, was sometimes as high as a dozen. When he wanted to reach beyond those, he would get Speed to hack into the MusicTVContinental cable system so he could pass major observations along to the whole world. In general, though, he tried to avoid crusading, although he did come pretty close it when the latest Hungry ("Feed Me Your Face") Pussy video came out and he got so worked up that when people actually went out and bought the Hungry Pussy DVD, they wondered where the scene was of the weird old man wagging his finger and thundering, "This is puke! This is pure, puking puke!" He had popped up in it every time it was broadcast on MusicTVContinental.

The Merricks also had their own line of videos and self-help books. *Fill Your Pocket$ with Million$ the Mrs.*

Marilyn and Mr. Murray Way. As she showed some of them to the executive committee, Sister Bernice explained that Mrs. Marilyn always hosted the show in her own beautiful home, where she would chat with clients whose homes the Merricks had sold and get them to talk about how much money they'd made on the deal and what they'd spent it on. Mr. Murray would appear as sidekick, and they always played up the love angle, how much they loved each other, and loved being together, and loved working together, and loved the money they made together, and all the things they bought with it. Mr. Murray would show off the motor yacht or the mansion in the Keys he and Mrs. Marilyn—it was how they always referred to each other, Sister Bernice said, and the way their names appeared under their photos, one on one side, the other on the other, of their For Sale signs—had purchased together this week.

"How do you figure they keep track of all their stuff?" Mt. Rushmore asked. "Some days I get up and can't find both my shoes."

Sister Bernice thought about writing "Shut up!" on her flip chart while she waited for everybody to stop rattling on about things they couldn't keep track of, except she had forgotten to bring a marking pen so she had to yell at them to quiet down instead. She observed that the committee appeared to agree that it wasn't greed exclusively or the general nastiness of the Merricks, which had been described often enough in the newspapers by employees who had been fired and tried to sue for back wages, or customers who felt they had gotten raw deals and sought amends and were chased away by the lawyers and armed guards who patrolled the Merrick real estate headquarters to keep Mrs. Marilyn and Mr. Murray safe. It was attitude. Specifically that the value of a person's life could be measured by what he could get for the property accumulated during it. Beyond that, though, there was every other attitude they displayed, all of them part of the overwhelming superiority that goes with accumulating riches.

Mt. Rushmore wanted to do it on the Merricks' TV show in front of the guests in the Merricks' beautiful home. He believed it would be a first, and would get big play worldwide. Sister Bernice said that was exactly the kind of thinking the committee had to avoid. It would just draw attention. She said the perfect execution would be one that nobody even noticed, apart from there being a body and evidence of foul play. The rest of the committee lined up solidly behind her, which Mt. Rushmore didn't take as a rebuke because he'd been having a hard time thinking of a way to meet their criterion of no muss and no fuss in a live—or even a live-to-tape—reality show setting. It was, on the other hand, relatively simple and perfectly appropriate to make it look as if her husband had done it after the background research unit discovered Mrs. Marilyn was banging Mr. Murray's psychiatrist.

According to the research unit's analysis, Mrs. Marilyn believed it made far better economic sense to bang the psychiatrist than to hire a private eye to track down what her husband did with the six credit cards he thought he had kept secret and to gather invaluable information for the divorce settlement she expected to receive when the time was ripe. It would also provide her with an early warning if Mr. Murray started to suspect that she was banging the senior group vice-president of Mr. and Mrs. Merrick Real Estate International, which she had been doing ever since he was a humble salesman who packed a wallop in his trousers. From the tapes the committee was able to acquire with the nifty new infrared microphone that could pick up voices from vibrations on the windows, she enjoyed the relationship with the psychiatrist, although it made the shrink feel insecure and unethical. Often he would weep for quite some time after she left, and was getting up two or three times a night to shower even though he had taken a dozen or so during the day.

Mrs. Marilyn Merrick was knocked off with what sounded to everybody on the committee like such an old gag they were sure they couldn't have dreamed it up. They must have seen it in a movie. As the Merricks got out of their Jaguar—"exited their vehicle," as Jimmy McDrool put it when he interrupted Sister Bernice during the briefing, derailing her train of thought. She stared at him coldly. McDrool, as well as a genius with electronic gizmos, was a stickler for the niceties of terminology, and his sense of technical correctness often helped ease the anxiety of newcomers who might worry that the committee's operations weren't as entirely secure and carefully run as possible.

"Where was I?" Sister Bernice looked down, as if the answer might be written on her shoes.

"In the basement of their condo?" offered Ballantine.

"Right," she said.

A masked woman, P. Tolemy, stepped out from behind a pillar with a snub-nosed Smith & Wesson revolver. She popped Mrs. Marilyn just under the left eye where, as Mr. Murray had shown off proudly on what would turn out to be the last episode of their show, the circles that had become visible were no longer, thanks to the liberal application of money to maturing skin. When Mr. Murray yelped in horror, a voice behind him said, powerfully and evenly, "Police! Don't move!" and a man in a trench coat and a fedora stepped from behind another pillar, levelling a pistol at the gunperson and showing Mr. Murray a police detective's identification badge. Ballantine was so sure that the sudden-appearance-of-a-police-officer-speaking-authoritatively dodge that he had dreamed up for knocking off Asshole No. 2 would work, even though he never did get a chance to try it out, that he said the trench coat and fedora were ridiculous and refused to wear them. At least until Chardonnay and London Derriere told him the wardrobe committee needed something to do, the same as everybody, so stop being such a prima donna. He didn't argue in the slightest about the latex gloves.

The detective strode boldly up to the gunperson and grabbed the Smith & Wesson. Then, turning to Mr. Murray Merrick, he said, "Here, cover me while I check the condition of the victim," and handed him the gun. Pressed it firmly into his hand. Shaped his fingers around the grip, his index finger over the trigger. And squeezed.

"Shit!" Mr. Murray cried, as a heavy round thudded into his wife's midsection, causing her body to flip like a fish in the bottom of a boat.

"Watch what you're doing!" ordered the detective, swinging the astonished Mr. Murray around sharply and squeezing the finger again, sending a round ricocheting wildly through the parking garage.

"Okay," the detective said. "That's enough. Let's blow this popstand," and started toward the exit. P. Tolemy beetled along after him. Mr. Murray, blubbering and aghast, stared at their departing backs and then at the gun, which he let drop as the detective stomped on the rubberized door-opener cable, and the pair disappeared into the sunshine.

It was P. Tolemy's first hands-on execution and she was elated on the subway ride back to The Cloister, but after a glass of champagne, she had to lie down and stayed in bed for two whole days. She wasn't upset, she told the debriefers, who came with fancy cookies and fruit juice and, as a memento, a rather fierce-looking teddy bear, although she got all teary when they presented it to her and snuggled it in the crook of her arm. She just felt tingly in all her extremities, tingly and light, as if she didn't lie down, she might fall over and float away.

When the question had been put to the committee that possibly Mrs. Marilyn Merrick had given Mr. Murray Merrick some pleasure in bed and, if so, would that not qualify as a redeeming virtue that would save her from execution, a transcript of the surveillance tapes yielded the following conversation.

Mrs. M.M.: I haven't let the son of a bitch lay a finger on me in years.

Mr. M.M.'s psychiatrist: So I understand.

ten

EVERY MONTH THERE WAS AN outing, and every month the guests at The Cloister were asked to suggest places they would like to visit. Sometimes somebody rigged it so most suggestions favoured the botanical gardens, but usually it was the racetrack or a casino—the racetrack because it had enough slot machines for everybody to work two. In fine weather there would be strong interest in the casino ships that cruised the waterfront—twenty dollars in chips and one cocktail included in the admission. No matter where the guests said they wanted to go, though, when the chartered yellow school buses dropped them off, it was at Total, the world's biggest discount store. So many outings from so many residential facilities went to Total that the buses had to circle, in holding patterns, while buses ahead of them dropped off their passengers.

"Hurry up, hurry up!" shouted the greeters, grabbing disoriented new arrivals and pushing them ahead to clear the way for the crowds piling up. "Come on! What's the matter with you people?"

The Cloister contingent was herded into the household products section where the special was four dozen double rolls of toilet paper for a dollar. "You can't afford to miss this, folks!" the herder shouted, prodding them toward the looming piles of toilet paper. "Hey, lady! Where the hell are you going?"

The greeters were funnelling people through the entrance so quickly the herders couldn't keep track of their groups. "Stick together in your assigned purchase section," they screeched through loud hailers, "or you will be placed in a time-out area until you start behaving like reasonable adults!"

Soon aisles were blocked with bundles of toilet paper that had been pressed into the arms of guests from The Cloister, who dropped them and tried to escape up the side aisles only to stumble over the heavy bulk packages of dairy-fresh non-creme topping and Spiffy Lube for all your automotive needs that had been dropped by guests from other residential facilities who were trying to escape.

A chipper voice rang from the public address. "Good morning, shoppers, and a total welcome to Total! This is your manager-in-chief." The voice had the clear assurance that comes with accepting deep discount as your saviour. "To welcome our special guests who come to us today from select residential facilities across the metropolitan area, Total is pleased to announce a one-time only offer. We have in stock more than 15,000 drums of dishwasher detergent specially labelled in large print. Look for the displays at the intersections of major aisles. Thank you, and good shopping!"

A second voice rasped from the public address.

"Maureen!"

It was definitely not the one that had been advising shoppers about the bulk detergent or, before that, the 144-tube packs of Gummy-Grip, the world's favourite flavoured denture adhesive, yours for just two dollars and fifty cents with the purchase of 1,000 super tampons.

"Shut the fuck up!" The scream was so thin it could hardly be heard five paces from the thin, bent, quivering screamer.

"Maureen! It is I!"

"Fuck you!" screamed Screaming Maureen, her shoulders heaving with sobs. "Fuck you, fuck you, fuck you!"

"Fuck you! Fuck you! Fuck you!" shouted her companions as they tried to keep her from falling and discovered they were chanting mindlessly along.

"Maureen! You spavined, dried out old cunt—"

"Fuck you! Fuck you! Fuck you!"

The chanting spread. Its essential rhythm galvanized the crowds that swarmed fitfully up and down the avenues of goods. The repetitive cries of frail voices had the menace of wind pushing a grassfire. The screamers felt an overwhelming need to flee the noise they were making, and the more they tried, the less they were able to.

"Shoppers! This is your manager-in-chief!" The clear voice had cranked itself up a notch, as if it was uncertain it could be heard. "We seem to have a problem with our communications system. Please bear with us while   "

"I don't know why anybody ever wanted to fuck you, Maureen," bellowed the other voice. "I never did. You were a duty fuck, Maureen."

"Fuck you! Fuck you! Fuck you!" Stumbling and falling, scrambling and cringing, throngs boiled along aisles until they collided with wild-eyed, terrified mobs coming the other way.

"Shoppers, please! Remain calm! We are trying to locate the source of the problem. In the meantime we ask everyone to respect Total's reputation by refraining from the use of foul language."

"Remain calm! Remain calm! Remain calm!" the voices clamoured. "Fuck you! Fuck you! Fuck you!"

The few customers still on their feet trampled over the backs of the fallen, crushing their ribs in the frenzy to reach the exits.

In the vastness of Total, one individual felt exalted as catastrophe swirled around him. Swept this way and that like driftwood, his glasses askew, his eyes glowing coals that lit his face with rapture, Mt. Rushmore raised his arms in wild thanksgiving.

"So this is what I want you to do, Maureen. Stick your head up your ass."

"Up your ass! Up your ass!"

"Shoppers, if you are not going to show proper respect, you leave me no choice. Attention, managers. Emergency stations."

A klaxon sounded. There were red, flashing lights. A recorded voice blared, "Managers to emergency stations" over and over.

Via the yellow emergency phones, the manager-in-chief told the managers that this was the most dangerous outbreak of shopper unrest in the history of Total. And the most obscene. He asked the managers to pray with him while he asked for guidance, and once he received it, he ordered the maintenance crew to immediately implement Section 57(b) of the Total Counter-Terrorism Defence Initiative.

"Amen," he said.

"God bless you, sir," said the managers.

After checking the *Counter-Terrorism Defence Initiative Manual* to refresh their memories, the maintenance crew, as instructed, threw the valves that opened the sprinklers.

As Mt. Rushmore felt the lash of mechanical rain, he let loose a mighty shout of exultation, and for a moment the whole of Total was illuminated by a brilliant, unearthly light that was extinguished only when the human undertow dragged him down and away.

The mountains of goods leaned, and then collapsed under the flood from the overhead pipes. Rescuers sorting the living from the trampled-to-death and drowned tried to see that the survivors were returned to the residential facilities they had left that morning, but it was hopeless. Often the victims who were able to walk were so shaken they couldn't make themselves understood. Others were in such shock they couldn't remember where they lived.

Many were delivered to wrong addresses, where harried staff installed them in whatever rooms happened to be empty. Ballantine estimated that as many as fifty of The Cloister's guests either perished or ended up in hospitals or other facilities, from which they never returned, and were replaced by others who were given the family photos and medicines and possessions of the guests they replaced and were expected to make do as best they could.

The next day, an exuberant Mt. Rushmore, who never missed an outing because he couldn't resist a bargain and believed that someday he'd find one, arrived back by taxi. One of his eyes was swollen shut and the lenses were missing from his glasses. "You should've been there," he hollered as he pulled Ballantine into the elevator. "It was a classic!" Bursting into his room, he grabbed the woman lying on his bed and dragged her into the corridor by the collar of his bathrobe.

"Keep the bathrobe, compliments of The Cloister," he told her.

"I never liked the colour anyway," he said to Ballantine as he climbed into his reclaimed bed. "And one of these days I'll show you what I got at the Total."

"You got something?" Ballantine looked around. Mt. Rushmore had been empty-handed when he reappeared.

"Up here." Mt. Rushmore tapped his temple.

"You got brain damage?"

"Go ahead, mock!" The wounded-to-the-core expression that was a Mt. Rushmore specialty couldn't compete with his exhilaration. "I'll tell you this. I was taken up to the mountain and I was shown the dance of death. The all-time killer dance. I saw it. And I learned it. And that's what I got us at the Total."

"A dance?" Ballantine wasn't sure he was following.

"Not a dance. The choreography. Yes, sir!" Mt. Rushmore punched the air with his fist, or he tried to. He winced and clutched his shoulder. "I got the choreography for the greatest monster mob-scene killer dance anybody can imagine. It's like I was present at the creation. Just wait. You and me, babe, we were born to dance.

"Now"—Mt. Rushmore shut his eyes—"I've got to get the mighty engine of my creative genius firing on all sixty-six cylinders again. Close the door quietly on your way out."

eleven

"FROM THE LOOK ON YOUR FACE, you must've loaded your drawers!"

Chardonnay ignored Banana's leer. She sometimes wondered if a loaded-drawers expression didn't slip naturally over her face when her mind was blank. It would have been understandable. Left to its own devices, her face would respond appropriately, and the sense of shit was everywhere. Many of the guests had accidents. Some had nothing but. One of the benefits of being a guest was that your olfactories were burned out by the time you arrived. More or less. The food in the dining room was so bland and overcooked that Chardonnay often asked why they bothered eating it. Why didn't they just dump it in the toilet? Cut out the middleman. It was wonderful to watch the faces of family members who had Sunday brunch in the dining room surrounded by mushers— what guests called guests who ate with their hands—and dribblers. The faint sewage smell rising from the steam tables, with the occasional ripe bouquet from a guest losing control on the other side of your son-in-law, could cheer all but the most clued-out through the still, windless shallows of a long afternoon.

But her mind wasn't blank. "It suddenly occurred to me—" she began.

"That you loaded your drawers?"

Banana could be irritating. But Chardonnay, as everyone knew, led him on. All her life she had been looking for a good straight man, and the choices were dwindling. The problem with Banana was delivery—even when he delivered a straight line, he did it *wammity, wammity, bam!* as if it was a laugh line. It threw her off her stride.

"No. It occurred to me what it is," she said.

"What what is?"

"The biggest joke of all."

"What biggest joke of all?"

"The one that's on us." She paused the length of an eyeblink while her audience—an audience was an audience—gathered his attention and concentrated it on her. Then she let him have it with both barrels.

"There's dick we can do about global warming," she said.

"That's a joke?" He looked pained. "I don't get it."

Chardonnay said, "I only just got it myself."

"Nobody can do anything about—"

"Not nobody. You and me. Us." With a sweep of her arm she included the whole building.

"That's funny?"

Chardonnay felt herself beaming. She felt as if she radiated light. That if she were suspended in the darkness of space, an astronomer would mark her down as a new star. She was surprised Banana wasn't shielding his eyes.

Because Banana could be irritating didn't mean he couldn't be irritated, and it irritated him not to get a joke. He went into the knitting ladies' sunroom. "Listen to this one," he announced.

"We're busy." The knitting ladies were always busy. "Come back when we're finished." The knitting ladies laughed out loud at this. They were never finished. The knitting ladies pissed off the other guests because the social workers and practical nurses were always finding things for the other guests to do—play beanbag or grow Victory Gardens on their windowsills. The other guests got in trouble if they didn't participate. The knitting ladies didn't. They were already participating their asses off knitting.

People approached them cautiously because they always made you feel as if you were interrupting something, which you always were.

"I can see that," Banana said when the knitting ladies held up their knitting to show him how busy they were. "But," he persisted, "I also see that even when you're busy you still have conversations. Ever notice?" The knitting ladies glanced at one another wondering what they'd done to deserve this cement-head. "Nothing but knitting permits people to be busy and have conversations at the same time."

"Like, for instance, when you're busy eating dinner," said a knitting lady, nodding.

"Or watching TV," suggested another.

"Walking."

"Driving the car."

The couches the knitting ladies sat on were starting to tremble.

"Buying groceries!"

"Brain surgery!"

"Cooking!

"Wait a minute!" one of the ladies shouted. "I got it—what nobody can do and talk at the same time! Sixty-nine!"

The other knitting ladies howled and whapped one another with their elbows.

"It was the only time he shut up, my husband," said a knitting lady. "I never got all that much out of it, but at least he'd stop talking, so what I got out of it was peace and quiet."

The knitting ladies bounced up and down, repeating the line. "Peace and quiet! Peace and quiet!" They wiped their eyes on the shoulders of their housecoats.

"I'm sorry?" Banana was getting nervous. Every now and then a conversation took a turn that made him feel not only that he wasn't in it, but that possibly he didn't exist. It didn't used to happen so much in The Cloister. It was why he was becoming less subtle as a straight man. He was starting to feel that nobody was getting set up by his setups. He was starting to feel as if he didn't get the jokes he set up, as if it didn't matter to some people whether he did or not.

"'Was it good'"—a knitting lady coughed and turned purple. "'Was it good for you?' my husband used to say. And I used to say 'Was what good for me?'"

Now all the knitting ladies were screeching and turning purple. "Was what good for me! Was what good for me!"

"Excuse me!" Banana was becoming exasperated. The knitting ladies looked at him out of the corners of their eyes, then down at their work.

"Please listen to this one."

They were silent except for the click of knitting needles.

"There's dick," he said, enunciating clearly so no one

would miss any shadings and nuances, "we can do about global warming." And waited for a reaction.

The click of knitting needles slowed.

"Do you get it?" Banana looked from face to face. "I don't either."

One of the knitting ladies bundled her needles and wool and stuffed them into her bag with the ring-shaped wooden handles. She sat for a while, pressing the tips of her fingers against her lips. Then she said, "I just remembered something," and levered herself to her feet. The others stood, too, the couches creaking as they rose. "Is it that time already?" one asked. "I had no idea."

The knitting ladies disappeared from the sunroom.

"Was it something I said?" Banana said. He laughed.

That line always guaranteed a laugh.

He wondered what it was he'd said.

Banana spent the next two days trying the joke on other guests. By the end of the second day there were no other guests to be found in the halls or sitting rooms. He was the only one who showed up for supper. Ambulance buses stood by in the driveway. Paramedics went up and down the corridors banging on doors and checking blood pressures and heart rates. Everybody seemed fine. Everybody just didn't feel like coming out of their rooms. Everybody just didn't feel like eating.

Ballantine got off his bed long enough to fetch a pad and a ballpoint. He lay back and wrote.

—Global warming

—Hole in ozone layer

—He closed his eyes and tried to recall some others.

—Spread of the Sahara Desert

—Nuclear disarmament!

—Running out of fossil fuels

—Star Wars (weapons in space) (Nuclear disarmament!)

—Clean water (not enough available for three-fifths of world to drink)

—AIDS

—Unequal distribution of food globally

—Genetically modified food?

—The population bomb

He left his room long enough to make photocopies and slip one under every guest's door, after which The Cloister became very still. It was now the third night since people had stopped coming out of their rooms or eating. Dental appointments had been cancelled. Everybody was feeling fine. Not unwell. Just strange.

But the next morning, the breakfast sitting was just about full. Lunch was packed, the biggest crowd the dietitians could remember when it wasn't Christmas. The dining room was afloat with laughter and excited conversation.

It drove Banana nuts. "What's so funny?" Whenever a table erupted with laughter, he rushed over and demanded to know.

The guests looked at one another and shrugged. "It's just—I don't know."

"We don't know either." Everybody would throw their hands up all at once.

"Who the hell knows?"

"It's like I can fly. I'm—"

"There's dick we can do."

"—free as a bird."

And they would laugh until their cheeks shone with tears.

Banana didn't get it.

"You're stuck somewhere," Chardonnay said.

"Where?"

"Back there somewhere. Successor worship. The most powerful cult in the country. You can't let go."

She counted off on her fingers. Everything must be done for your children. If you didn't do everything possible, you feel guilty. If you didn't have children to do everything possible for, you feel guilty. If you did everything possible for your children or the children you didn't have, it wasn't enough. You feel guilty. And it isn't just material things. It's security, it's ambition, it's courage, it's health. If any of them don't have any of that stuff, it's because you screwed up.

"You never," she tapped Banana on the chest, "got over it—worrying about what kind of world you were going to leave your grandchildren."

"You didn't worry?"

"Of course. Everybody did. That's not the point."

"What's the point then?"

"That's the point!"

"What is?"

"What's the fucking point is the point!"

Banana felt as if he was writing an exam but didn't know what the subject was.

"What is the fucking point of worrying about things we can't do anything about any more?" Chardonnay said.

Had grandchildren ever taken the world left to them

by their grandparents and improved it? Hadn't they always just fucked it up more royally?

Banana rallied to their cause. "Some of them took what they inherited and made fortunes."

"Did they make a better world?"

"They made a better toilet." Banana was grabbing for something to hang on to. "And the world beat a path to their bathroom doors."

"So we should idolize them?"

"If we don't, they don't visit. They don't phone. They—"

Chardonnay grabbed Banana by the nose and pulled him toward her. "If you're ever going to make it as my straight man, you can't sneak in gag lines that were old when the first amoeba crawled ashore."

The knitting ladies surprised everybody by going on the offensive, setting up barricades and a checkpoint at the front door. Aggrieved children of guests were astounded. Many were in their fifties and sixties and felt deeply sorry for themselves for having aging parents they had to visit. They couldn't understand why they weren't being let in to do something they didn't want to do in the first place. The knitting ladies were in no mood to explain. "We're busy," they said. "Go away."

For days, only staff was allowed through. "Why won't they let us in?" the children pleaded as staff members were having their I.D.s checked by the knitting ladies. The staff refused to comment. They had been advised that if they said anything without prior approval from the knitting ladies, it could lead to an outbreak of everybody shitting all over the place. Somebody snuck into a social worker's office during the night and shit on her telephone. The knitting ladies called this "an indication of good faith."

What got them to lower the drawbridge was a document written by Black-Eyed Susan and Chardonnay who had both been lawyers and were equally adept at resoundingly obscure prose. It said that Whereas and Wherefore and Notwithstanding and Nolle Prosequi and Ipso Facto the undersigned guests refused hereinafter to take any credit or blame for the state of the world they bequeathed to their heirs and their heirs' heirs and so forth.

"What it means," Black-Eyed Susan explained at the rally where everybody signed, "is that effective immediately we will no longer be accountable for history. More significantly, we cede ownership of the future."

"In short," said Black-Eyed Susan, "we're telling the world to fuck it."

"I don't get it," Banana said.

It was then that Chardonnay started to suspect Banana wasn't going to get much of anything any more.

It was the next morning that Ballantine woke to find that somebody had been into his room and left something in the middle of the oval rug in front of his dresser. A videotape.

It showed him slipping his list of things they couldn't do anything about under the doors of all the guests. It had been assembled using tapes from the security cameras on each floor. Somebody had put considerable effort into splicing it together.

twelve

SPEED WAS PISSED OFF when Ballantine said it reminded him of pinball. It wasn't anything like pinball. It was like a computer game.

"Think of it as the first computer game with real blood."

Ballantine didn't want to think of it.

Ever since Fastrack had put The Cloister up as collateral for a loan from an offshore bank in Vanuatu, things were moving in ways he couldn't always get a grip on. In the succeeding days, guests working in Fastrack's boiler room took the Vanuatu loan and moved the money to the Channel Islands, to Liechtenstein, to Latvia, to the Caymans, each time getting more credit against it.

"You'll see," Fastrack said when Ballantine asked why.

"Voonootoonoo. I never even heard of the place," Speed said.

"Van-you-at-too," said John Dillinger, raising a despairing eyebrow. John Dillinger told everybody she'd been a high-school principal. This surprised exactly nobody because even when she didn't happen to know something, she said she did in such a way that nobody was prepared to argue. Fastrack didn't care whether she knew anything or not. All he cared about was whether she had the balls to mastermind the hit that would demonstrate to international financiers that The Cloister was a major player.

Speed said she'd done that all right. "She laid out the mattress for whacking Abu Badali."

"Matrix," said John Dillinger.

Abu Badali was scurrying from five-star hotel to five-star hotel, making them worry that he knew they were on to him. They didn't realize that if he knew they were on to him, he would have stopped scurrying long enough to say, "What can I do for you?" Life as an arms merchant had its risks, but life as a home appliance dealer had its risks, too, and Abu Badali always hoped somebody was on to him and took it for granted that they could find him, otherwise how would he sell them weapons? The only reason he scurried was that he was a scurrier.

Sometimes, though, if you scurried this way when you should have scurried that way, your body would be found with your testicles stuffed up your nose. Naturally it was assumed something along this line had happened in Alexandria when Abu Badali's body was found with his testicles stuffed up his nose, prompting the authorities to attribute the death to natural causes.

His problem was that John Dillinger and Speed were new to the game.

"It was easier than I expected," Speed told the committee.

He was so excited and proud that he kept flicking the joystick of his electric wheelchair, twirling around in the crafts room where the executive committee had gathered to find out why two black cars full of men with heads like giant boiled cabbages were parked out front, keeping track of comings and goings.

"Run over my foot again and I'll smack you," said John Dillinger.

"Right," said Speed.

"Just calm down." John Dillinger fixed her gaze on each member of the executive committee. "The folks here seem to think we've done something wrong."

Speed was speechless. The way they'd knocked off Abu Badali had been brilliant.

"Maybe they'd care to tell us why they think that," she said.

It would be wrong to say John Dillinger scared Mt. Rushmore, but if she didn't, she did make his guts go all jangly.

"I don't believe she's a dyke," he told Ballantine.

"Four children, she told me. Two husbands."

"Three," Mt. Rushmore corrected. "Seven grand-children, two great-grandchildren. I don't take anything for granted any more. If there are facts, I find out what they are."

"You've found out more facts about her in the time she's been here than you have about guests who've been around for years, and she doesn't even sit at our table."

"I think she wants to run the show."

"There is no show."

"I think she was born with a whistle around her neck. Any minute she's going to blow it and tell us all to play volleyball."

"There is no show and nobody runs it." Ballantine knew this for a fact because everybody thought Ballantine ran it, and he knew he didn't.

"Some women who are very authoritative, they come across as dykes."

"How do you know about her husbands and everything?" Ballantine asked.

"I surfed the Net."

Ballantine looked at the newspaper in his lap. Newspapers sent unsold copies to residential facilities like The Cloister.

"I hear she wants us to march into the dining room," Mt. Rushmore said.

The newspapers wanted to show they had valuable things to offer the marginalized. The newly arrived copy on Ballantine's lap was only ten days old.

"If she wants to run the show, fine," he said. "Nobody's going to stop her."

He turned a page.

"Before dinner, we'd form groups. Each table. We'd march in. Or roll. Limp. Hobble."

Ballantine figured if he waited long enough, he could stay out of the conversation.

"It might be interesting," Mt. Rushmore said finally.

Speed was pointing out that they had dealings with so many offshore banks because Fastrack had the boiler room keep The Cloister's mortgages in constant play when he was interrupted by Sister Bernice who asked how they could take out a mortgage on The Cloister. They didn't own it. Didn't they have to show somebody a deed? Speed couldn't believe his ears. "When you've got the kind of talent we've got here, it is no problem coming up with a deed."

"I should have known," said Sister Bernice.

"And when you get that kind of dough snowballing, and international operators constantly in need of cash infusions," Speed said, "the banks get pretty competitive regarding customer services."

"You mean like free chequing?" asked Chardonnay.

"And specialists who can track down potential clients or even people who owe you dough and have gone missing. This one specialist in England was named Colonel Alf. He and John Dillinger got along so well that Colonel Alf even tossed in a few 'extras'. Abu Badali getting offed sent an important message to some important individuals to the effect that The Cloister wasn't playing patty cake." Speed looked around.

"You don't think we should've whacked him?"

"We don't think anything," Sister Bernice said. One or two other committee members nodded, apart from several whose heads always nodded. "We were just interested."

"You just wanted Speed to bring you up to speed," said John Dillinger in a sardonic tone that made everybody a little clammy in the armpits.

"Never preach, never teach," Sister Bernice said as she plopped down beside Ballantine. "Is that right?"

It was the Evening Cookie Club and Ballantine was trying to peel the plastic cover off a package of crackers and cheese food. He'd put money in the machine and pushed the button for a Mars bar, but a package of crackers and cheese food wound up in the pickup bin and he'd long since given up arguing with this machine. It gave you what it wanted to. Other guests had warned that this week it was promoting crackers and cheese food, but Ballantine had forgotten or he wouldn't have put his money in. He could never open the packages of crackers and cheese food.

"Do you think they were just showing off?" Ballantine asked, patting his pockets for something sharp that he could jam through the plastic.

"I guess we should be happy they didn't knock off whoever runs China these days. Do you want me to open that?"

Ballantine pushed the package away. "No thanks. It would spoil the aggravation."

"It makes me think of Angel-Eyes," Sister Bernice said.

Ballantine sighed. Sometimes he grew tired of half measures. So had Angel-Eyes. She used to take the fire axe off the hook every time she got a prescription from the drugstore and chop the bottle to pieces to get at the pills. As she grew older, though, it wasn't just the child-proof tops that defied her. It was swinging the axe. The next time a prescription was delivered, she pulled the fire alarm. An hour or two later a firefighter, who looked like an intergalactic frog in his breathing apparatus, poked his head in Angel-Eyes's door and told her she should evacuate. She said nonsense, and handed him the bottle she couldn't open.

Stern warnings were issued. Angel-Eyes's children were called in. They were shocked that their mother would do anything so irresponsible when she couldn't afford a bed elsewhere and they might be forced to take care of her themselves. Angel-Eyes said she had learned her lesson, and the next time a prescription was delivered, she had her city councillor and two TV crews on hand when she pulled the fire alarm. It made the news on four networks that night, and several national publications wrote no-bones-about-it editorials: If the drug companies weren't such major contributors to political parties, unfortunate individuals like Angel-Eyes could hope for change.

The dining room buzzed for weeks as guests tried to guess what revenge Dixon would take on Angel-Eyes. It would have to be pretty subtle considering that her new national prominence pretty well guaranteed she would have a place at The Cloister forever. Then, when Angel-Eyes upped and died after breaking her hip on the stairs during a fire drill, the dining room buzzed about what revenge Dixon would take on all the rest of them to make up for the revenge she had been denied by Angel-Eyes's departure.

Angel-Eyes hadn't been showing off. "She was just doing what needed to be done," Ballantine said, but Sister Bernice had gone. He must have fallen asleep. He wondered if there was anywhere he couldn't fall asleep as long as it was daylight. That's probably why he woke up. It had grown dark.

She hadn't been there long when it became clear to the other women that all the men in The Cloister had the hots for John Dillinger. The slightest attention from her thrilled them. They lined up just so they could be told to go away and stop bothering her. This pissed the other women off. Novelty was novelty, and every new arrival turned heads; for days men's voices would be deeper than usual. And they would be far more interesting than they had been within living memory. But after a while things settled back to normal. Men sniffing after a newcomer would discover she smelled bad. Men looking for companionable reverie in the sunroom would discover she was a disciple of the Vita-Soy Diet ("Carry the bloom of youth to the very end") and wouldn't shut up about it. Men looking for a piece of ass like they thought they remembered having decades ago would discover she hadn't had sex for thirty years and wasn't interested in starting up again. Men looking for a bridge partner would discover she couldn't keep track of trump. Men looking to feel needed would discover she could keep perfectly busy without their input. Men looking to feel appreciated would discover she thought they were ineffectual. Basically, men would discover they were no longer necessary, which they had been discovering for some time and didn't need to have confirmed again. It was known as the Petering Out Principle. It had been proved over and over. Until John Dillinger showed up.

Ballantine didn't respond to John Dillinger the way the other men did even though he had been prone to giddiness in the past when a new woman guest moved in. Ballantine was being battered by entirely different feelings—competitiveness and insecurity. What did he care if she wanted to run the show when there was no show to run? And why did he worry that if he didn't watch his ass, somebody would stick a hand grenade up it and pull the pin?

Maybe it was because she made it clear she didn't like the way he didn't run things. Maybe it was because he told her that if she thought she could do it better, she should go ahead, he didn't give a shit. But she refused to take his not giving a shit as an admission of defeat. Maybe that was why the fast one she pulled threw him for such a loop that his immune system collapsed and he ended up coming down with the cold that was almost the death of him.

No guest had ever been given a testimonial dinner. No one had ever thrown a testimonial dinner for Ballantine. That someone would do it at this stage of the game flustered him. The dinner called for endless arrangements, and John Dillinger took care of them all. She was in the administration offices ten times a day, and came out checking off items on her clipboard. There were going to be decorations. Skits. The theme would be "The Man Who Has Given Us Something to Live for." There would be a special menu. Everyone would dress up. Everyone would march into the dining room.

Ballantine was flattered and appalled. He was appalled because he hadn't given anybody anything at all. He had simply done what he thought needed to be done. Other people had done the same thing. He played no more of a part than anybody else. But how could he turn down the honour? Most people don't get any honours. Ballantine never had. And you needed to have received plenty of them to have developed the know-how to turn one down. Having no experience at all left him without an alternative. Even if he'd wanted to say no, he had no idea how to do it.

Then he discovered he had to make a speech. He had never made a speech. He had no idea what to say. It made him sick to his stomach. He spent hours every day making notes, writing drafts, reading them in front of his bathroom mirror. He'd awaken in the night, convinced that everything he'd written was even worse than he'd thought, and he'd tear it up and start over, losing sleep, growing hollow-eyed and pale. Finally, when he was sure he had something worth saying, he tried it on Mt. Rushmore, who smiled and said, "That's fine."

"Fine?"

"It's the same bullshit everybody says at one of these things. It's the same bullshit everybody expects to hear. That's what it's supposed to be. That's fine."

Ballantine was devastated and started over. He was turning into a basket case.

Sometimes what he wrote looked ahead to what the world might become if people became more actively involved. Sometimes it looked back to what his life had been like before he became involved in it. Sometimes he just laid out the facts for his audience to reach their own conclusions. Sometimes he listed the conclusions because he was sure that nobody else had reached them. The more he worked on it, the more bombastic he sounded. The more pompous. The more strident. The more foolish. The more like the complete asshole he had always dreaded becoming.

He decided the only approach was total humility. He'd simply tell his story from beginning to end and leave it at that. He tried it on Mt. Rushmore, who smiled and said, "That's fine."

So Ballantine set out to do better—a man who had never given much thought to his life striving to extract

from it what had been important, what had been conse-
quential, what had meaning, what had worth, what he'd
learned, what he'd discovered, what would be useful to
others. A man who had spent his life in wholesale fruits
and vegetables could make a difference! Here was how it
happened! Here was Ballantine stripped bare!

There was silence when he finished speaking. For
almost a full minute there wasn't a sound in the dining
room. No one had expected him to sit down so quickly.
They wondered what was going on. Had they missed
something? They had put up with all the pre-testimonial
crap for weeks and now they were looking for a return
on their investment. You could taste the expectation
when Mt. Rushmore introduced him as "The man who
truly has given us all something to live for."

So no one knew quite how to react when Ballantine
stepped in front of the microphone and said, "What I'd
like to say is this: Always put the fresh on top."

And that was all.

When the room finally exploded in cheers after the
stunned silence, it was like a wind that threatened to
blow Ballantine over. Mt. Rushmore was holding a hand
toward him and shouting, "Take a bow, take a bow!"

Ballantine stood and bowed, buffeted by adulation.

And when he left the stage he was immersed in it.
Hands shaking his hands, squeezing his shoulders, ruf-
fling his hair.

"Congratulations. That was wonderful. Shortest
speech I ever heard."

"I was afraid we were going to have to sit there all
night."

"So short! Great!"

"Good for you for not dragging it out!"

"What was it you said again—'Down in front'?"

"Fresh on top," Ballantine said.

"Was that it? Terrific!"

He sought out Mt. Rushmore and put it to him directly. "You can hardly say that was the same old bullshit," he said.

"Sure it was," Mt. Rushmore said, throwing his arms around Ballantine. "Just shorter."

Ballantine lay awake for a long time that night, trying to figure out whether his feelings were hurt. He couldn't make sense of what he'd been through. But eventually, this feeling of being on a boat that was rolling and tossing him around even though the water was calm gave way to a chill sense of sinking. What had he been doing up there? Was he out of his mind? The last thing he wanted to do was draw attention to himself. But he'd let it happen. He had let John Dillinger hang him out in front of Dixon. And leave him there to spin.

Just as he was thinking he'd have to lie very, very low, a trickle of phlegm tickled the inside of his nostril and he sniffled. Jesus! Now he wasn't going to have to lie low, he was going to have to go into hiding. When morning came, there was no sign of Ballantine except for all his belongings.

He was catching a cold, his life was in danger, he was on the run.

thirteen

"I DON'T THINK she's a dyke," said Chardonnay.

The knitting ladies nodded in agreement. Chardonnay had found Ballantine snoozing in the sunroom and shaken him awake. He was so newly returned to the world after living on the run and obtaining a new identity that he wasn't used to being recognized. When people spoke to him as if he was the Ballantine they had known for ages, he had a panicky urge to pretend he had no idea what they were talking about.

"What are you talking about?" he said.

"Stop screwing around." She dragged him to the doorway and gestured with her chin. "There. See what I mean?"

Ballantine was stumped. "No."

"If it walks like a dick…" She looked knowingly at him. He looked at her. They looked at the distant figure of John Dillinger.

Ballantine said, "You mean like a duck?"

"And talks like a dick…" Chardonnay's pauses were dramatic.

"Like a dick?"

"And hangs around with—"

"Dicks?"

"—dicks."

"You're telling me she's not a dyke." Ballantine was perplexed. "That she's—a duck?"

"A cop." Chardonnay crossed her arms and stared narrowly at John Dillinger. "That's what I'm telling you."

As far as Chardonnay was concerned, it explained everything, not the least of which was why John Dillinger was having a big old chat with that guy over there.

"What's that guy got to do with it?"

"He's a cop."

"Really?"

"It sticks out all over."

To Ballantine he just looked like an old guy. Not that old, but getting there.

"That's probably why you haven't noticed him," Chardonnay said. "He sort of looks like somebody who's checking the place out like he's thinking of reserving a spot. He's been hanging around for a couple of days."

Ballantine had been preoccupied with other matters, but nobody on the executive committee paid much attention to security. If they got caught, the operation would just shut down. It wasn't a big deal. What was anybody going to do to them?

Mt. Rushmore refused to believe they had been infiltrated. He refused to believe his fascination with John Dillinger might be a subconscious response to her not being what she appeared to be. He liked to think he found her attractive for what she was—a somewhat masculine, extremely bossy old lady. And for her enthusiasm. When you started taking what you did for granted, having somebody come along who found it—and, by extension, you—exciting, it put a spring in your step.

"Not a spring, exactly," he said.

"You were pretty enthusiastic once," Ballantine said.

"Maybe she's been a little too enthusiastic."

It wasn't like she jumped up and down. "She was interested. She wanted to help."

"She helped quite a bit with that Abu Badali thing," Mt. Rushmore reminded him. "That whole craziness."

"They always do that," Sister Bernice said. The men slid their chairs back so she could pull hers in. She had a paper plate of cookies. "In books. Spies. Undercover operatives. Do some of the dirty work just to make everybody think they're one of them."

"See?" Mt. Rushmore glared at Ballantine, justification blazing from his eyes. "What did I tell you?"

"That's exactly what I told him," Chardonnay told Mt. Rushmore the next morning when she decided to stop hemming and hawing and march right up to John Dillinger and say, "So who's your new boyfriend?"

But when she spotted her at breakfast, she sidled up and said, "That guy you were talking to yesterday in the Concourse. I saw him out there again just now. Probably looking for you."

John Dillinger sat up very straight, raising her eyebrows, and appearing very surprised. "Really?" she said.

Chardonnay thought for a minute that John Dillinger was going to come all over flustered, maybe even blush. But she didn't. So Chardonnay said, "What is he, a relative or something?"

"No," John Dillinger said. "He's a police officer."

Chardonnay had to concentrate very hard to keep from dropping her tray and yelling, "No shit, you double-crossing bitch!" She had to concentrate very hard to make sure all she did was smile sympathetically.

"You don't suppose he's on to us?" John Dillinger asked.

By mid-morning, the whole executive committee was asking itself the same question. Ballantine mulled it over as he watched to see whether anybody showed up to collect the guests who had been dumped on the sidewalk to make way for that morning's contingent. "Out with the old, in with the old," he said to himself. He knew it was simply attrition. Not even the guests in The Cloister could die off or catch colds quickly enough to make room for all the potential guests clamouring for places. These guests had been hauled out there for running out of money, or because their pension and care plans had dried up or gone bankrupt. They could be a painful sight, especially in foul weather when they were drenched and wind-chilled blue. New guests who took pity on them, smuggling out blankets or bits of food, were warned by guests who had been there longer that sidewalks were closely monitored by the administration, and guests who let charity get the better of them had ended up on the same sidewalk too often for it to be a coincidence.

Mt. Rushmore's voice boomed behind him and Ballantine would have jumped if he wasn't so used to Mt. Rushmore coming up behind him and booming something.

"We're going to do something about that one of these days!" Mt. Rushmore was scowling over Ballantine's head at the rousted guests. "It can't be allowed to go on."

They'd been through this many times. Some things were out of the hands of ordinary people, and particularly guests of The Cloister. The folks on the sidewalks represented a management decision, and messing with management was like messing with the cosmos. The whole thing might come flying apart.

"Shitting on the social worker's telephone. That wasn't messing with management?"

"Just a little reminder that we're here," Ballantine said. "But that out there"—he nodded toward the sidewalk—"that's a matter for management."

Mt. Rushmore humphed.

"Come on," Ballantine said. "I'll buy you a jug of prune juice."

"No. I'm raging."

Ballantine, looking at the guests who had been tossed into the lap of fate with their pathetic possessions, agreed. "It's tough all right," he said sadly.

"No. There's nothing we can do about that. I'm raging because the woman who has been disturbing my dreams turns out to be a cop. They talk about the enemy within? Well, I got the enemy"—he pointed his finger at his head like a pistol—"within me. I'm sorry, but I can't talk any more. My thoughts are being monitored." And he raged off.

The dumb old bastard. "You shouldn't be dreaming at your age anyway!" Ballantine shouted after him. But all he got back was the finger.

Ballantine's own enthusiasm for the work of the committee waxed and waned, and when it waxed, it never seemed to shine as brightly as it had before, although he didn't trust his memory entirely. Maybe—and when he thought about it, it was certainly possible—he had never been terrifically enthusiastic. If he was fully occupied with something worthwhile and necessary, such as earning a living, would he be devoting his time and energy to knocking off the world's bastards? As for that, the benefits of murdering people who deserved to be murdered were mostly selfish. You do something, therefore you are something. If he didn't murder them, he would no longer exist. He had never been motivated before by anything beyond housing and feeding his family and revenge after the death of his wife. What did he really care that Miles G. Concannon presented a target of opportunity? Every rational person with even an iota of humanity would agree that Miles G. Concannon was a deserving target. What Ballantine wondered was whether anyone who could even vaguely be called rational would take advantage of the opportunity.

"I would never have been doing this years ago," he told Jimmy McDrool.

McDrool thought about this.

"And you wouldn't either," Ballantine said.

McDrool thought about this too. "Maybe that's because it never occurred to me."

"Is it just because Concannon's rich?" Chardonnay asked at the committee meeting.

"It's because he's here!" Speed shouted.

The meeting was shocked into silence. While none of the members believed in beating around the bush, speech this direct still took everyone's breath away. The silence was becoming oppressive until Speed broke it. "I mean he will be. On the twenty-third."

A relentless heaviness remained in the air. Before Speed and John Dillinger had demonstrated The Cloister's global reach by whacking Abu Badali, all the nominees had been within reach of public transit—one of the committee's central principles. Apart from that, they had been rich. Those finally approved for execution tended to be very rich.

"Bad people who are poor tend to be in custody." Mt. Rushmore said this in a tone that suggested he wasn't exactly sure what it had to do with anything.

"Rich people sometimes go to jail," said Sister Bernice.

"Did anybody ever think that maybe if we talked with them they would get the message?" John Dillinger asked. That wasn't particularly helpful in the circumstances, but then for all her helpfulness, some people were thinking maybe she wasn't all that helpful.

"And what exactly would our message be?" Ballantine asked. He was always trying to get everybody to agree not to send a message, even if they knew what it was. Once he'd said, "We do not dance in the end zone," then spent the next twenty minutes explaining to the knitting ladies that it wasn't smutty. Many murderous organizations obviously wanted to leave messages: The Irish Republican Army, the Hells Angels, the Mafia, Al Qaeda, the Central Intelligence Agency. Their murders had to do triple duty, the second of which was to warn others to cease and desist if they didn't want to end up in the same state. The third was to show just how fucking scary they were.

"Why would we want to kill Miles Concannon?"

"Look," Sister Bernice said, "we already voted on it."

"Just doing what we can," Mt. Rushmore said, giving Ballantine a little verbal goose. "And him we can do."

Yep. That was it. Miles G. Concannon was someone they could handle. And so they would kill him. And that's all they wanted from life. They weren't trying to impress anybody. They...

The next thing he knew, McDrool was poking him and telling him it was bedtime.

"It doesn't do any good," Ballantine grumbled, beginning the laborious process of becoming upright, "teaching anybody a lesson if they're not around after to benefit from it."

fourteen

BOROFSKY DIDN'T LIKE LOOSE ends. One of the loosest ever was the official departmental firearm—a Glock nine-millimetre automatic pistol—found where the sniper had set up to shoot Miles G. Concannon. The Glock was already a loose end and this made it even looser. It had been issued to a police officer named Amy Wheatcroft, who had, in the course of her career, become part of a large new demographic within the department—soccer moms. Then she became part of a much smaller demographic—officers who quit the force and went into real estate when they realized their career was going to be nothing but bad shifts and no promotions after they reported their service weapon missing. Amy Wheatcroft's story had rocketed to the top of the charts among cautionary tales in police colleges, but Borofsky was the only one who, more than two years after the fact, still spent time wondering what had become of her gun. He thought this was probably because he didn't have a whole lot else to do.

She'd had the weapon, holstered, loaded, along with her notebook, walkie-talkie, handcuffs, extra ammunition, pepper spray, and the other regulation equipment at inspection when she started work that day at noon. At eight that evening, when she and her partner finally got a break for coffee, she didn't. Her partner noticed her holster strap was loose when they got out of the car.

Officer Wheatcroft discovered that not only was the strap unsnapped, the holster was empty. This had become a permanent loop in Borofsky's thoughts and kept running even when he was unaware that he was thinking about it. In the supermarket he would discover he was hefting two pounds of butter just to get a tangible sense of how much you ought to notice when the weight of a Glock is no longer on your hip.

There may be worse things that can happen to officers than losing their service weapon, but short of using it to blow away the police chief, not much. Even losing it when an armed perpetrator gets the drop on you and relieves you of it and runs away is pretty much a career ender. Because the police department fostered teamwork and selfless dedication and ideals of the highest honour and duty, and because brotherhood was the unwritten code, every member of the department was always suspicious of every other member. None of Amy Wheatcroft's colleagues was absolutely certain she hadn't sold her gun to buy drugs, although to do so would be incredibly shortsighted. Drug fiends aren't careful planners, though, and every officer knew a dozen ways to beat the drug tests that had pronounced her as clean as a whistle when she insisted on being retested right after her loss. But they all thought it far more likely that she "arranged" to lose it so her lover could pass it along to a button man on the Coast who needed a weapon that couldn't be traced to organized crime. Her lover, part of the Mafia's wide-ranging intelligence operation, would have insinuated himself into her life to keep track of what was going on inside the force. Then he'd mentioned he needed a gun for "self-defence" and disappeared the minute he got hold of it, leaving Amy Wheatcroft heartsick as well as crazed with remorse. None of her girlfriends on the force knew of her having had even a date for dinner and a movie, much less a lover, and if anybody would know, they would. She and her police girlfriends spent a lot of time together outside of work, carpooling and arranging baby sitters and bitching about their ex-husbands. All any of them knew was that she'd been pissed off because the shift her gun disappeared was an extra one she'd been stuck with and meant she wouldn't be able to get to her daughter's swim meet. "Soccer mom" was a generic term; Amy Wheatcroft was actually a swimming mom.

"Pissed off," Borofsky wrote in his notebook. "Wrapped up in own problems." "Not thinking clearly." "Not concentrating."

One entire folder in the file contained a long reconstruction that began less than two hours after the weapon was reported missing, roughly the time it would have taken her to get back to the station and fill out a missing weapon report. Police officers who aren't liars and cheats keep a more precise accounting of their time than anybody but lawyers. Lawyers do it to justify their billable hours; police officers do it in case they have to testify in court and need an alibi. Wheatcroft and her partner were able to go step by step through everything they had done preceding her terrible discovery, just as she would go through it four more times officially as she carried out what amounted to an investigation of herself, and then fifteen more times with no more success until her therapist told her she was exhibiting obsessive tendencies. Wheatcroft denied this, although in the four months since the weapon vanished, she hadn't been to a swim meet or a piano recital—she was also a piano mom—or had sex with the guy she was banging, whom she hadn't mentioned to any of her girlfriends because he was separated from one of them. She hadn't even changed her clothes because she believed that the memory of what happened was somewhere in or on her being and she risked losing the information if she lost direct physical contact with it. She slept in full uniform, including her steel-toed uniform shoes, and became quite a sight, and pretty smelly. By the time she came to be known as "the bag lady of 53 Command," her ex-husband had successfully sued to gain custody of their two daughters and had taken them to live on the other side of the country, where he was followed by Wheatcroft's very best girlfriend on the force, who had been banging him for years.

So Borofsky wasn't entirely prepared for the tremendously fat redhead who drove him to lunch in her tremendously fat BMW after he told her on the phone that her gun had been located at last. "Holy shit!" she'd said. But then Borofsky was never entirely prepared for any of the ex-cops he met, even the ones who had put in their twenty years and retired, which he'd been unable to bring himself to do. "Unwired" was the word he used. No matter what, they all seemed unwired. He would never have described them this way to anybody else; neither would he have told anybody what he meant by it since it struck him as kind of bullshitty. It had to do with those stuffed birds and flying dinosaurs he remembered from the museum when he was little. They were held up by wires. They were wired.

What Borofsky wanted from Amy Wheatcroft was exactly what he got—nothing. All he asked was whether anything had come to mind, something she had somehow forgotten or overlooked during the months that followed. Nope. Not a thing. So it had to be somewhere in that file, and the only thing in there that had been overlooked, at least relatively, was the old lady. She'd been sent off in the ambulance two hours before Amy Wheatcroft's firearm was discovered to have disappeared.

He presented The Cloister's administration office with her name, insurance numbers, and the date of her transfer from the convalescent hospital. He informed the staff that he wanted to talk to her about certain matters that had arisen concerning her estate. Was he a relative, he was asked. No, he was a police officer and showed them his badge.

This is what intersected with John Dillinger's prudent cultivation of the administrative staff. She had carefully planted the notion that being informed about people who weren't relatives asking unusual questions about guests was in everyone's best interest—they might be expressing particular curiosity about a guest's condition because of a possible inheritance, they might be criminals or have criminal intent, or they might be representatives of financial organizations that would dynamite the guest's financial underpinnings and leave both the guest and The Cloister in an awkward and unsatisfactory position. John Dillinger believed it was entirely practical for the executive committee to have its own intelligence apparatus and, given the sensitive nature of the information that might be collected, believed there was no need to inform the committee that the apparatus existed. And here, hadn't it paid off?

So who wouldn't have been suspicious to find her talking intimately with Borofsky, especially when you were already suspicious of her? Even Borofsky was suspicious. He had hardly been invited to take a seat and wait while the administrative office looked into the situation regarding the guest he was inquiring about when an extremely self-confident old lady sat down beside him and began asking him pointed questions in the oblique fashion of a police officer who wasn't on official business exactly, but was conducting general inquiries. At first he thought she must be the old lady he'd come looking for, the only character in the Amy Wheatcroft story who was never interviewed directly. Considering the Wheatcroft old lady's age and injuries and her raggedy drift through the hospital system, she had seemed irrelevant and had disappeared from all but the typed departmental record. But Borofsky had, along with time on his hands and a niggling curiosity, an insatiable desire to irritate his commanding officers by showing them to be pretty much the sorts of morons they thought he thought they were.

"It's because I've been around too long. I make them nervous," he told Ballantine a few days later, after the fuss his appearance caused had settled a bit.

His appearance the day after he'd identified himself at

the desk and asked to see V8, however, was prompting a good deal of goddamning from John Dillinger, who was uncharacteristically ruffled.

"He wasn't supposed to come back until he got a phone call," she said to Chardonnay. "And he hasn't got a phone call yet. You don't suppose he's on to us?"

"Why didn't you tell us about this yesterday?"

"I was going to."

"And?"

"And I forgot."

"*You forgot?*"

John Dillinger looked deeply into Chardonnay's eyes. She squeezed Chardonnay's hand comfortingly. "It happens," she said.

John Dillinger told the administration office that if they could possibly arrange for the police officer to come back at 11 a.m., everything would work out in everyone's best interests. By that time the committee had smuggled V8 up to a private room in the round-the-clock-care section of the gaga floor and briefed her about what to expect when her visitor showed up.

"Why would he think I had the gun, dear?" she asked John Dillinger, who was tucking her in.

"Maybe it has your fingerprints on it."

"My fingerprints!" Happiness transformed V8's frightened face. "Of course." She looked at the tips of her fingers, buffing them slightly with her thumbs. "Fingerprints. How wonderful!"

She was alone when the door pushed open slightly and Borofsky slipped through. She was lying on her back. Her eyes were fixed on the ceiling. Her jaw was slack. Her arms, outside the sheet, lay limply at her sides, palms down, fingertips discreetly out of sight.

"What did you do with the police officer's gun?" No hello. No nothing.

Borofsky thought the good cop–bad cop routine was a bunch of shit and in any case he was alone, although if he'd had a partner along, he would have insisted their routine be bad cop–bad cop.

V8 didn't move. Except to breathe.

He said it again.

He walked to the side of the bed and leaned over so his face was directly in her line of vision. She gave him a smile that flickered like the sun off water. She licked her lips with a tongue as dry as her lips were.

"I have to go home," she said. Her voice was fragile. She lifted a hand as if to touch his face, but stopped halfway. "Will you help me? Will you bring my clothes? I have to go home."

Gagas were always trying to escape. They wore tracking devices that set off an electronic signal if they wandered beyond their perimeter. They believed—for many it was the closest to a cogent idea that remained in what was left of their faculties—they were prisoners.

"The lady police officer—"

"Will you help me?"

"—who came to your apartment." Borofsky spoke each syllable distinctly. "When you fell and hurt yourself."

"I have to go home."

"You took her gun."

"Will you bring me my clothes?"

"What did you do with the gun?"

"You could take me home."

Her tragic derangement would have melted the door of a safe. Borofsky narrowed his eyes. The corner of a folded newspaper was sticking out from under her pillow. There was a ballpoint pen on the night table. The paper was folded open at the crossword puzzle. Detectives could spot things like this because they spent a lot of time doing crossword puzzles. And Borofsky could spot Alzheimer's because he'd spent five years watching it turn his wife's brain to bird gravel. "If that's today's crossword," he said, "eleven down is 'Kemo Sabe.'"

"I have to go home."

He spelled it. "What Tonto called the Lone Ranger."

"Will you help me?"

"I just did."

"Diddy-dum, diddy-dum, diddy dum dum dum. Diddy—" V8 launched into the William Tell overture. Borofsky could still hear her dum-diddying when he waited for the elevator. He picked a newsletter off the rack and flipped through it. It was put out—what, every two, three months?—by the guests. The headline "Notable Passings" caught his eye.

Maybe it caught his eye because in a place like The Cloister, where there were passings every day, there was only one item. It read, "Guests at The Cloister were interested to acknowledge the unfortunate death of Lorenzo Metcalfe." That was it.

"I'll be fucked," said Borofsky.

For years, Lorenzo Metcalfe had published books, although recently he had devoted his energies to maintaining several Web sites that, like his books, denied the

Holocaust, described the threat posed by the Jewish conspiracy, and reminded readers that the demonic seed planted by Martin Luther King, Jr. and fertilized by left-leaning governments was growing tall and hardy. Recently he had been found floating face-down in an aeration tank at one of the sewage-treatment plants along the waterfront, although the cause of death turned out not to be drowning in shit, but Drano found in his system in a concentration high enough to stop the engine of a bulldozer. Somebody had shot him full of the stuff.

When Borofsky showed the newsletter to the reception desk and asked if back issues were kept, he was directed to the reading room where, after rummaging, he found all kinds of them in a cupboard under the bookshelves. "Notable Passings" started about a year ago. He recognized five of the names from unsolved homicide cases. Something about all this washed through Borofsky's veins like a sweet and powerful tranquilizer. When he woke up, he was stretched out on a couch and an attendant was telling him to go into the dining room or he'd miss dinner.

"No, no," Borofsky said. "I don't live here."

"Of course you don't," said the attendant, with weary condescension. "Come on, I'll take you in."

It pleased Borofsky that he was still quick enough to outrun an attendant in an old folks' home. "Abu Badali," he found himself saying as he started the car. "Abu Badali."

Where the fuck had he heard that name before?

f i f t e e n

"You know *Crime and Punishment*?"

Whatever Ballantine had been expecting, it wasn't this. "No. Never read it." He wondered what he had been expecting. Goddamned if he knew.

"Me neither," said Borofsky.

"I don't read a lot," Ballantine said.

"Me neither."

"The paper. That's about it."

"I'm the same," Borofsky said.

He had on a light topcoat—a raincoat, unbuttoned—although the sunroom was warm. He sat forward on the easy chair, his feet splayed, his knees spread, his arms dangling between them. He was tall enough that his fingers just about touched the floor. It was an odd pose, half collapsed, half poised to jump up. Detectives don't wear hats any more, but Ballantine had the feeling that if this one had worn a fedora, the brim would have been turned up at the front.

"What is it?" Borofsky said, glancing at his watch. "Eleven o'clock. In buildings like this, climate controlled, I always get sleepy about this time of the morning. It's the same at the office. Actually, it's the same everywhere. I'll be driving and I'll have to pull over because— boom!—I'm as good as asleep. So I guess it's not just the building. A nap helps, or a cigarette. Coffee doesn't any more. You don't smoke, do you? I figure nobody probably does in here. I almost don't. I mean, now I feel the urge, but it'll pass if I—if I have a nap, it'll pass for sure. I can go days. Unless I have a drink or two. Then I just say fuck it and smoke. Why fight it? The danger is you start having a couple of drinks every day just so you can smoke. Hey! I guess the danger is you start drinking at breakfast so you can. Maybe before breakfast. Jesus. I can hardly believe I used to smoke before breakfast. You too? First thing I did when I woke up. Light it right there on the edge of the bed. Even before I took a leak. Un-fuckin'-believable."

His voice sounded peaceful, low-pitched. It didn't carry far. It made Ballantine think of a quiet, aimless conversation in a bar with an acquaintance, neither of them in a rush or with much to say, but comfortable saying it.

As if remembering how that cigarette before breakfast tasted, the cop made a cartoonish grimace and looked out the window for a long time. Then he held his hand out to Ballantine. "Borofsky," he said. "And you're Mr. Ballantine."

Yes and no. But he would know that. That was probably the point. "Ballantine," Ballantine said. His throat was froggy. He had to cough to clear it.

"Ballantine." Borofsky nodded agreeably. He leaned back and looked around. Guests in the sunroom looked quickly away. "Funny how the idea of a place like this used to give me the creeps. Now I almost get the feeling that living here wouldn't be a big problem."

Ballantine gave a halfways wink. "You're a bit young."

"I fuckin' wish." Borofsky leaned forward, more or less rolling to his feet, then stooped and banged his kneecap with an open hand. He spoke to it. "Come on!" He looked at Ballantine. "I don't stand up all at once any more. Anyway"—finally unbending his knee and standing erect—"I got to go. I'll see you around."

"Jesus!" Mt. Rushmore said after Ballantine recalled as much of the visit as he could. "What do you suppose that means?"

"I guess it means he'll see me around."

"Jesus!" said Mt. Rushmore.

Borofsky slumped behind the wheel. He couldn't remember the last time he talked so much non-stop. He was never much of a talker, but since his wife got sick, there hadn't been anybody he wanted to talk to. Big Red, his girlfriend, took care of pretty much both sides of their conversations. And he was tired of talking to cops. Every conversation he had with a cop nowadays sounded exactly like every other conversation he'd ever had with every other cop. He really wanted a cigarette. That was fucking insane. He hadn't had a cigarette for fifteen years. Maybe he'd go have a drink. That was fucking insane. He hadn't had a drink at lunchtime for almost as long.

Ballantine must have been asleep. The TV set was on, but he had no idea what the show was. He thought it was ridiculous to go to bed before nine unless you were sick, but he had a hell of a time staying awake until nine unless he was working on something. Somebody was at his door. That must have been what woke him up.

"Coming!"

Borofsky looked at Ballantine, then looked at the card

in the holder on the door. "I thought this was the right room number, but the name—"

"There was a little mix-up. I thought they'd have replaced that by now."

"D. Keith Finton," Borofsky read.

"He was going to move in here, but then he didn't. So when I heard it was available, I—"

"A change is as good as a rest," Borofsky said. "Listen, you got a minute? It's not too late?"

Would Borofsky like a drink?

"No. Thanks. I saw the light under your door. Thought I'd say hello. What is that? Rye? No shit. I don't remember the last time I drank rye. Okay, a small smash. Hm! It's funny. You know they say smell is the biggest jolt to your memory? Like just now I'm remembering the last time I drank rye. No. Not the last time, the first time. Drank it with ginger ale. Can you believe that? I get the same smell thing when I go to the firing range. Not that I go any more. At least I haven't for a long time. It's too fucking gung-ho these days. I don't even have a goddamn gun any more. I mean, I have one, but I don't carry it. It's in the car. That's probably stupid. No, it *is* stupid. Some kid steals the car, he opens the glove compartment. Holy shit! A car, a gun—he's on his way to being a master criminal. But what if he jumps me? Goes for my wallet? Says, hey, what's this? Gets my gun and my wallet. Like I'm going to be able to fight off some big fucking kid. Or some little fucking kid.

"Look at that." He holds out his fist, thumb cocked, index finger extended like the barrel of a gun. There was a wobble. Not quite a tremor. "You fucking believe that?

They see me on the firing range, everybody runs for cover. It used to be that what you wanted wasn't so much to shoot straight as not to scare the fucking shit out of yourself when your gun went off. Now everybody's got these yellow glasses and soundproof ear things. Helps them concentrate on their aim. Who the fuck has time to aim? And everybody standing there with the butt of their gun planted in the fist of their other hand, like in the movies. Everybody wants to be a movie star. Nobody's happy with being just, you know, normal."

He was sitting the same peculiar way as in the sunroom—feet splayed, knees spread, arms dangling. "Those pictures on the dresser? They your relatives?"

"They're uh—"

"Fintons?"

Borofsky was out of his chair and stooped over with his nose almost touching the pictures, as if he needed reading glasses.

"You don't miss much," Ballantine said.

"Actually," Borofsky said, holding out his empty glass for Ballantine to refill, "I do. Cheers."

Something about the way he paused made Ballantine expect they were about to take off on a tangent, but Borofsky said, "I was talking about memory. Smell or something. Anyway, whenever I'd go into the firing range, the smell of gunpowder would make me think of every time I ever fired my gun. I mean in the line of duty. All six of them. Twice I missed. That leaves four I shot. One guy I missed slipped out of my hands hanging out a window. Now *that* was like the movies. Four is a record, I think. Probably for the whole Western world, if you don't count cops in Argentina mowing 'em down with machine guns. Not a thing of beauty, any of them. Every one I emptied the whole fucking gun into them, or at them anyway. You don't go bang and then stop to see if the fucker is still coming at you. You want to stop him for sure. *Really* stop him. One less witness, you know what I mean? Not that what you're doing isn't right, isn't what had to be done—your life threatened, or the public endangered. I mean, you're the only one who knows when your life is in danger. It's easy for somebody else to say it wasn't, for the guy who was about to blow your head off to say that's not what he had in mind. Must have been a misunderstanding. I figure there are five times I wouldn't be here if I didn't have that misunderstanding. It's not like shoot first and ask questions later. It's like make sure you're still around later. The first one I missed, he disappeared around the corner. I think I fired probably five shots after he was out of sight. You get carried away. You just keep fucking shooting. And the other guy, he got so scared he jumped out this window. We were in this hotel room. I don't blame him. Bullets flying everywhere. I'm shooting, he's shooting. We're both scared shitless. So his gun jams and he climbs out the fucking window, only there's no ledge or anything. He's holding onto the sill by one hand, got his other elbow hooked over it. He's looking over his shoulder like, what the fuck do I do now? I say, oh for fuck's sake, and grab him by the wrist, and I get my other arm around him, and he kind of relaxes a bit now I got hold of him. Then I think, 'You fucker, you were fucking going to kill me,' so I let go. We're on the sixteenth floor. He was a police officer. I'd known him for years. A complete fucking asshole. Today they investigate the shit out of you. Shoot your gun in public, you get investigated by the KGB. You don't even have to shoot anybody. Investigated, counselled. To make sure you're not some kind of homicidal maniac, or you won't commit suicide because you blew some fucker away. Okay, I can see if it's maybe an accident. But when you're serious about shooting somebody and you shoot him, what's the fucking problem? It's like you selling fruits and vegetables. What did you do after you sold them, have a nervous breakdown? That's the business you're in. That's what happens."

Ballantine wondered how Borofsky knew what business he'd been in.

"Holy shit, look at the time. Listen, thanks for the drinks. You've given me a lot to think about. And good-night to all you Fintons." He flipped the photos a salute. "What do you figure, some of those must be great-grandchildren. Maybe I'll get to see your pictures sometime."

"You gave him a lot to think about?" Mt. Rushmore shook his head.

"I didn't say more than two words the whole time."

"What do you think?"

"Goddamned if I know."

The front door had been locked, so Borofsky hit a crash bar and went out the fire exit. He was about halfway to the visitors' parking when a voice stopped him. "Excuse me!" It was the attendant who'd been dozing at the reception desk. The man was breathless and appeared uncertain. "You're—you're not a guest here are you?"

"No," Borofsky said. "I've been visiting one of your patients."

That seemed to confuse the attendant even more.

"Is something wrong?" Borofsky asked.

"They—uh, the alarm. Some of the guests wander off and get lost. We put a thing on their ankle, so they can't sneak out. It rings the alarm. Did you sign out?"

"I didn't sign in."

"Oh." The attendant was backing up slowly. "Maybe there's something wrong with the alarm."

"I'll be fucked," Borofsky said, slipping behind the wheel. He pulled up his pantleg, undid the holster strap, and tossed the Baby Glock on the seat beside him. He sat for a few seconds massaging his ankle where the phantom weight remained.

It was two days after the astonishing thing about V8 had been on TV all day and everybody was still talking about it and about the different things they'd read about her in the newspapers when Borofsky came into the dining room. He stopped behind Ballantine and said hello around the table. Everybody said hello back.

"I got to kill some time before a meeting," he said. "Mind if I catch lunch with you?"

Everybody made jokey gacking sounds. "Gosh." "Sure." "Taking your life in your hands."

He came back from the steam table with a little bowl of green Jell-O, a little bowl of fruit, a cardboard carton of milk, and a plate of whatever it was.

"Not probably what you're used to," Sister Bernice said, eyeing Borofsky's tray. "We were just wondering what anybody might guess it was who hadn't seen the menu board."

Borofsky studied his plate. "Chicken something?"

There was mumbled laughter. "Dover sole à la king," said Mrs. Don't Touch Hutch.

Borofsky gave her an inquisitorial look and she started to laugh. He said, "At the police station I work out of, McDonald's has the cafeteria contract. This has got to be better."

"Bo—" said Mt. Rushmore, trying to remember Borofsky's name.

"Sometimes Bo. Sometimes Bobo. I used to get Bobo a lot starting out, but most of the guys I started with are gone."

"I was getting at," Mt. Rushmore explained, "whether you were a Sergeant Bo or a Captain Bo or what?"

"Just plain Detective Bo. I've been a few other things. I was a superintendent for a while, till they discovered I didn't superintend anything. I always wanted to be something like police commodore."

"What about archbishop?" said Mrs. Don't Touch Hutch.

Borofsky laughed. "Archbishop of detectives."

"Has a nice ring," said Jimmy McDrool.

"Unless somebody confessed to him," Ballantine said. "He'd have to keep it a secret."

Borofsky pointed his finger at Ballantine and flicked his thumb: Good shot.

"Whatever you are, Detective Bo," said Sister Bernice, "you don't sound like—pardon me for saying it—one of those Irish policemen whose father was a policeman and his grandfather before that."

"Detective O'Bobo," Jimmy McDrool said.

"You sound like some kind of cop yourself," Borofsky said as Sister Bernice watched him. "My old man was a doctor." He tapped the bridge of his nose. "Eyes. I got led astray. Actually I was getting led astray by lousy marks, but one summer—late one summer, we were supposed to leave the next day to go back to university."

They got very drunk, and the next day they were very hungover, but they remained true to the solemn vow they'd sworn the night before—to make the world safe for women and children and broads with big tits and the poor and the oppressed. And to kick the fucking shit out of the fucking bad guys. They signed their names on each other's wrist in draught beer. And showed up at the police station to fill out application forms.

"What happened to your buddy?" Mt. Rushmore asked.

"Made deputy chief." Borofsky said as if the proposition surprised him. "Seemed to like all the chickenshit. A good deputy is good at chickenshit. A politician, really. You need your own constituency. His was real estate. The real estate industry. Nothing like a cop for a go-between at City Hall. It's not what most people expect. When a cop comes by your office and says such-and-such a real estate deal is good for the city, politicians listen kind of differently. He did pretty well. Retired at fifty-four when he had the numbers. And the cash."

"It all sounds—"

"Unsavoury." Sister Bernice finished Mt. Rushmore's sentence.

Borofsky shrugged. "Not everybody has a rich doctor for a father to leave them enough money to stay honest."

He walked out of the dining room with Ballantine, but stopped when they got to the elevators. He pushed the button. "I've got to see a lady about a gun."

Jesus Christ! Now what? "That lady you were in to see a while ago?"

"Uh-huh. Got something that might interest her."

"She—uh." Ballantine tried to look composed, except he couldn't remember what he looked like when he looked composed. "Didn't—I guess nobody told you?"

"What?" Borofsky looked composed.

"She died."

"Died?"

"Passed away."

"When?"

"A while ago. She hadn't been very well. She was, you know—" Ballantine made a woo-woo circle around his ear.

"Aw. I'm sorry."

Mt. Rushmore was aghast. "Doesn't he watch the news on TV?"

"I don't know."

"Ran it over and over all day. It was all over the papers."

"I don't know."

"You keep fucking saying you don't know."

"I don't know."

"You do not know."

"I don't know."

Borofsky didn't even bother pulling out of the parking lot. He slid the seat all the way back, stretched out, and closed his eyes. Being the life of the fucking party was wearing him to a frazzle. Then he sat up, rummaged in the glove compartment, and pulled out a videocassette. Sometimes when you're sixty-four you think you know exactly where you put something, but then you have a minute's panic. He looked at the label he'd written. "Old lady strangles Hungry Pussy (Wheatcroft gun)." He stretched out again and closed his eyes. Fuck he was sleepy.

sixteen

JIMMY MCDROOL HAD an unusual skill for someone who had been a druggist for forty-seven years. He
had invented a device that would open the electronic locks on automobiles while disabling the theft-
prevention system. Maybe it was because for the last
fifteen years his drugstore was across the street from
a plaza that had 358 parking spaces and a People's
Discount Drug Warehouse open twenty-four hours a
day. When he wasn't counting the parking spaces, he read
the magazines on his rack, particularly *Practical
Electrical*, which he still subscribed to in an on-line version in The Cloister. He'd got quite a bit of information
out of it over the years—some helped him come up with
the unlocking, theft-prevention-disabling device.

This remained nothing more than a conversation
piece until the day the magazine ran an article about igni-
tion systems. After a bit of trial and error in Muppet Labs,
Jimmy McDrool could not only open almost any vehicle
without it screaming bloody murder or going into fully
frozen, all-wheels-locked inoperable mode, he could start
it and drive it away. For an encore, McDrool's machine
also turned global-position-system satellite trackers to rat
shit. He kept these developments a secret until the
moment he could invite his pals to take a gander out
front, where, under the portico at the entrance, right up
on the sidewalk, its bumper snubbed tight against the

glass doors, sat a brand-new midnight blue Eldorado he'd driven off the lot of the biggest Cadillac dealer in town. It sat there for several days, making it impossible to get in or out the main entrance, until McDrool called 911 anonymously and the police towed it.

He told the executive committee that this technology would save the costs of public transit. The committee reminded him that their executions were for the good of the world, and the candidates were actively destroying every bit of good they encountered. Stealing a car, however, was theft.

He said they didn't understand. It was more like borrowing, since he would always report its whereabouts as soon as they had finished with it. He had no intention of keeping the cars. He had no place to keep them. And selling them would be complicated and risky.

Ballantine said he thought the biggest risk would be driving. And not because of the chance of getting picked up, but because of the chance of knocking somebody down. Collateral damage. This hurt McDrool's feelings. He, for one, was as capable of driving as when he first got his licence at sixteen. Exactly, Ballantine said. McDrool said, exactly what? Okay, Ballantine said, but driving without a licence was an offence.

To show he was as good as his word, McDrool would head out in the morning, steal a car, and drive it to within walking distance of The Cloister, then phone the police and report its location. Sister Bernice cautioned him that if he kept using the same payphone, the police would stake it out, but McDrool had thought of that and made his reports from a bunch of different payphones. It worked like a charm until one morning the police operator said, "Hey! The Volvo you reported yesterday wasn't there when we—"

McDrool had the presence of mind to hang up, but he was rattled. Either he had forgotten where he left the Volvo and given the police the wrong location, or some son of a bitch had stolen the car he'd just stolen.

There was only one thing to do. Be scientific. Recreate the incident. Ideally, of course, he should have stolen the same car again, but since he couldn't, he found an identical one on the same dealer's lot. He took Moom Pie with him to corroborate his evidence. She had never stolen a car before and found it quite exciting. Was this what they called joyriding? McDrool said he didn't think so. Joyriding involved getting burgers and shakes. Scoring drugs. Moom Pie said she wouldn't mind a burger and a shake, but McDrool was intensely task oriented.

"I've never ridden in a Volvo before." Moom Pie was admiring the interior. "Is it true they're from Sweden?" McDrool had never spent much time with Moom Pie. Since turning up a year ago, she had written up the newsletter's social notes, so he assumed she was vapid. She certainly sounded vapid this morning. He got the feeling she would find riding an escalator exciting. When he'd cast around for somebody to take good notes so he could be absolutely certain where he ditched the car, John Dillinger said there was no way she was going to ride around in a stolen car with somebody who didn't have a driver's licence.

Black-Eyed Susan mentioned Moom Pie, whose interest had been piqued by the committee meetings she had sat through and had asked if there was anything she could contribute. Since McDrool's problem was as straightforward as any that had come along, he might as well give her a whirl.

Moom Pie smiled back at the scenery. "I once had a dress the same colour as that awning when I was in high school. I wore it to my graduation. It becomes me, that colour. Teal blue. Did you ever wear anything teal blue?"

McDrool didn't answer. He was looking for a spot near where he'd ditched the last Volvo to ditch this one.

"My goodness," said Moom Pie. "I've never parked in a no-parking zone before."

"Now we'll find out if it's true about a criminal returning to the scene of the crime," said McDrool.

"You just did," Moom Pie said.

McDrool stared at her for a while. Then he said, "Never mind. Write down exactly where we are. We'll watch the car from that doughnut shop."

She thought it looked like quite a nice place and was very pleased to see it had washrooms. And a doughnut and an apple juice would be every bit as lovely as burgers and shakes.

At the counter, McDrool tried to keep an eye on the Volvo and get somebody to serve them. Two women wearing smocks and aprons and baseball caps with the doughnut chain's logo moved back and forth, taking orders. Moom Pie was knocked out by the decor—wasn't McDrool amazed that innovative business enterprises never fail to find unique decorating schemes that personify their products and trademark personalities? There had to be a million doughnuts on the wallpaper, photographed so clearly they were almost three dimensional. She asked whether McDrool had ever seen so many doughnuts in his life, but he wasn't listening because the women had gone up and down the crowd at the counter twice, and when it happened a third time and neither had offered to serve McDrool, he figured it wasn't just one of those accidents that sometimes happen in retail.

"It's why they have those Please-Take-a-Number gadgets," he said loudly.

"Who has what?" Moom Pie asked brightly, trying to place what he'd said in the context of her adventure.

"Take a number. Butcher shops and like that."

The women behind the counter served the person right beside McDrool and then looked at the customer on the other side and asked what they wanted.

McDrool was getting so upset he was forgetting to watch the Volvo. When he rapped sharply on the counter and shouted, "Hey! How about some service?" both women gave him dirty looks.

The other customers glanced at him, then looked away.

"It's our turn," McDrool said. "We were here before all these people." Things like this happened to him a lot these days. He'd go somewhere for a cup of coffee and by the time he caught the attention of the server, his nerves were so jangled he didn't need the coffee.

"Here you are, sir." The woman's voice was clipped as she dumped their orders on a tray.

"And how much will that be?" McDrool had an urge to add "my good woman," but he couldn't even be bothered to jack around any more, even in self-defence.

"I don't know, sir," the woman said. She pointed to a sign over her head. "Order here." "The cash is down there." At the far end of the counter a sign said, "Pay here."

"If you go—"

"Holy shit!" McDrool yanked Moom Pie toward the door.

For Moom Pie, the surprises just kept on coming. "Are we leaving now?"

"Hey!" the woman behind the counter yelled. "Hey, you fucking old fucks! Where the fuck you going? You fucking old fucks are all the fucking same. You come in here and fucking cause—"

There was a little flatbed truck beside the Volvo. While one man used some gizmo to open the car's door, the other worked some levers that tipped the flatbed like a dumptruck, lowering its tail to the pavement. They hooked a cable to the Volvo, hauled it up, levelled the load, and drove away. Elapsed time? Later on McDrool estimated forty seconds.

"This way!" He pressed his electronic device. The door locks of a Buick SUV clacked. McDrool put his shoulder under Moom Pie's butt to heave her up into the passenger seat, and scrambled behind the wheel.

"Woo-hoo!" she said.

"Keep your eye on that truck."

"Follow that car!" Moom Pie shouted. "That truck! That car on that truck!" She had high colour in her cheeks and her eyes were gleaming. "It's like in the movies!"

She was looking through a pair of tiny binoculars. "They're heading on to the expressway! They're heading on to the expressway! Get into the right lane! Get into the right lane!"

Where the fuck had she gotten binoculars?

They exited the expressway in a warehouse area.

"What are they doing? What are they doing?"

Was Moom Pie saying everything twice, or was he so pumped he was hearing everything twice? The truck turned into a maze of corrugated-steel sheds and shipping containers the size of semi-trailers stacked eight or ten high, but when he followed, it was nowhere in sight.

"What do you think? What do you think?"

McDrool had the feeling that this would be a reckless time to go gaga, and willed himself to concentrate. "Shush!" he said to Moom Pie. "Shush!

They crept up and down between towering stacks of containers. When they finally saw the little flatbed, it was no more than fifty paces ahead and the two men who'd been in it were out talking to a man beside a hulking tanker truck that was coiled with what looked like fire hoses. Nearer, and walking toward McDrool and Moom Pie, were a dozen people, all Asians, all armed. Wrong. Just one of them was armed, and he gestured with some kind of machine gun for the others to squeeze past the SUV. Except for him, they all looked weak and filthy.

"He says he's got to hose out the container those people just arrived in."

McDrool's head snapped toward Moom Pie. Her voice had taken on the efficient tones of a telephone information recording. She had something in her ear, and what looked like a little flashlight pointed at the men ahead of them. "He doesn't know what container they're supposed to put the Volvo in."

"What *is* that?"

She kept her eyes on the men. "A thing they advertise on television for hearing conversations on the other side of the room. Remote-Aid, they call it. Not available in stores. It's not great. With a good parabolic mike I could count their heartbeats. At least it's daytime, so we're okay without night-vision goggles."

Maybe he was going gaga anyway, McDrool thought. Maybe he'd already gone.

"But this is fine for checking out the lunch someone's husband is having with a bimbo. Somebody's supposed to tell them"—she slipped back into information-recording mode. "The hose-truck guy says whoever was supposed to tell them went somewhere after they opened the container and saw everybody was still alive. Told him to bring the pressure washer around and hose the thing out. He thought maybe this was him in the SUV."

The man pointed toward the SUV.

One of the other men said something that looked to McDrool like "Who the fuck is that?" and ran around the front of the truck.

"What did he say?" McDrool asked.

"He said, 'Who the fuck is that?'"

The man came back carrying a handgun. McDrool dropped it into reverse and stomped on the gas. There was a racketing burst behind them. The Buick lurched. There was a second burst. The Buick lurched again. He saw the man with the machine gun standing in the middle of the lane.

"Not a good move," said Moom Pie.

McDrool was terrified. "What?"

"Shooting out our tires."

"What?"

"He should've taken us out. How did he know we didn't have something like this?" She pulled an enormous pistol out of her bag.

"What the fuck is that?" McDrool's voice was barely a squeak.

"V8's Glock. I told her I was going to begin a life of crime, and the darling gave it to me." She jacked the action open and shut, ramming a round into the chamber. She slipped the safety off. Then, as smooth as water, she opened the door and wheeled to the ground. Her stance was square, her grip two-handed.

Pop!

It was the loudest pop McDrool had ever heard. Pop! Again. "Get out here!" Moom Pie dragged McDrool across the SUV console and behind the SUV. The guy with the machine gun was lying on his back.

"They'll have to think what to do now. We have the initiative for a minute."

"Did you learn from the movies? How to—"

"In the mountains. My husband was a believer." Her late husband believed that God helped those who could sustain themselves when the government failed them, which it had been doing for decades, or when it became a dictatorship, which it was becoming. He and Moom Pie spent a number of summers in the Rockies at a militia training camp.

"Lovely times." Moom Pie smiled and peeked around the fender. "Nothing but organic food and wild game."

"You learned to shoot like that?"

"It's pretty basic." She examined the Glock thoughtfully. "It's no rocket-propelled grenade launcher."

There was no sign of the men who'd been in front of them. Just the truck with the Volvo on it and the truck with the hoses.

Moom Pie studied the terrain, cover, light conditions.

"Why didn't you go back there?" Time for McDrool hadn't slowed down, and it hadn't speeded up. It had split. One time was going on between those other people and him and Moom Pie. Another was going on between just him and Moom Pie. It was as if they had plenty of it.

"After he died. Why did you pick The Cloister?"

"I didn't pick The Cloister. I wound up in it."

That was something McDrool knew about.

"And I did go out there." Moom Pie's eyes were moving along the upper edges of the stacked containers. "They said, 'Sorry. We have to stay mobile.' I said I still get around pretty good—I could cook or something. They said, 'Sorry.' I say we go for the truck with the Volvo."

"What?"

She was dragging him again. She fired three more shots, ricocheting rounds off the steel doors of the topmost containers.

"Give them something to think about," she said, and pushed him up against the side of the flatbed. He felt its idling vibrations against his cheek. "It might be standard transmission," she said. "Can you—"

Something whanged through the door she was opening, something like a giant bee. She turned and fired twice. One of the men from the flatbed fell on his side. The other had dropped to his knees. He fired once without aiming, then tipped forward on his face. Moom Pie slid to the ground beside McDrool, a red spot the size of a quarter on her cheek. He tried to set her upright, but when he reached around to hold the back of her head, he got a handful of mush and blood.

"Gimme that fucking thing!"

The hose-truck guy came flying, knocking McDrool sideways and reaching for V8's gun. McDrool grabbed something hanging off the side of the truck and swung it like a baseball bat. It was a long brass nozzle, and it was connected to a hose, and when he hauled back to swing it, it snagged a valve or something. Water shot out the end with such a jolt that it dumped McDrool on his ass. But the momentum of his swing carried the stream of solid water across the hose guy's neck, slicing through it as easily as if it was a dandelion stem.

The hose guy's head tipped to the side and fell on the ground. The rest of him remained standing for some time before collapsing in a heap beside it.

McDrool let go of the hose, which squirted the windshield out of the Volvo. He picked up Moom Pie's bag, put the Glock in it, and walked slowly through the maze of containers until he came to a driveway that led to a road. He slipped around the gate and walked until he came to a payphone. He called 911 and reported the location of his latest Volvo and the Buick SUV. He apologized for the windshield in the Volvo.

seventeen

JIMMY MCDROOL REPORTED Moom Pie's death to the Clean & Tidy Brigade and handed Ballantine a package to be returned to V8. When Ballantine said that maybe McDrool ought to give it to V8 himself and tell her how much he appreciated her lending it to Moom Pie since it saved his life, McDrool said he would rather not. V8 would want to have a big discussion and he, frankly, didn't want to talk to anybody for a long time, and certainly not about what the other guests had started calling the Gunfight at the O.K. Intermodal Shipping Terminal.

There had been a big splash in the news. Four dead— three males, one female, elderly, all unidentified. One male beheaded, the other three deaths by gunshot. Evidently the result of a war between international car-theft rings.

The following day, a new guest was installed in Moom Pie's room and the Clean & Tidy Brigade asked the newcomer if she would be interested in taking over Moom Pie's family. The Brigade had discovered it could make a few bucks by offering bereaved families first dibs on a replacement guest. Often very little effort was required. The family was already uncomfortable about visiting an elderly relative who might do something really disgusting while they tried to make small talk in a room that, even when freshly painted, smelled like shit.

If the Brigade hit it just right, they were able to offer the family some comfort by intimating that if they treated this replacement as their nearest and dearest, it would wean them of their guilt. If the family agreed, the usual Clean & Tidy Visiting Relatives deal kicked in—a set fee paid to the Brigade and split with the participating guest. If the departed guest's family didn't happen to notice the substitution, the arrangements were oblique. The replacement guests would request a few dollars to get their hair done or to chip in for a wedding gift for one of the nursing assistants. All income was split evenly between the participating guest and the Brigade. The Brigade's take, minus expenses, went to the executive committee for its work.

Screaming Maureen had run the Brigade very effectively until her late husband started taunting her about his sexual exploits in the afterlife. As the former chief elder of a large Presbyterian congregation, Screaming Maureen knew how to squeeze every last cent out of an emotionally difficult situation and had no compunction about asking astonishingly direct financial questions. With the harassment causing her more distress by the week, however, Christmas in July had taken over and, thanks to her Tupperware background, expanded the visiting operations beyond the families of guests and departed guests to neighbours of The Cloister who might enjoy having a Clean & Tidy relative for long weekends or special holidays like Thanksgiving or Passover. She organized block parties, bringing two or three available Cloister guests. The neighbours could choose the temporary relative best suited to their situation. The most obvious benefit was that the supervision provided by the Brigade ensured that, should a contract relative become aggressive or less than clean and tidy, they would be quickly removed and, if the family wished, replaced with one more appropriate.

Ballantine gave the Glock to V8 and said, "You probably wondered where this was."

"I gave it to her precisely in case something like that happened," V8 said.

Ballantine envied how assured people were about their association with the work of the committee and wondered if it had to do with the way they had started out. While he felt considerable satisfaction in achieving what he originally set out to accomplish, the way he'd done it had been so clumsy that guilt often threatened to make him lose control of his bowels. This was because the assholes died by accident rather than by design. There had been design, but their deaths were the results of flaws in the design. It was impossible for Ballantine not to feel sorry for somebody who died accidentally, even if he had been trying to knock them off at the time.

Nobody at The Cloister bought it when he told them that the score he'd rung up as a solo operator was unintentional. No, "unintentional" wasn't the word. The intention had been there. There had been serious premeditation, but they all died by fluke. Ballantine never came right out and admitted that he felt guilt, and it never occurred to any of the other guests that he did. The deaths of the assholes had been the executive committee's original inspiration. They were the foundation murders.

Everybody assumed that Ballantine had operated in the same spirit as the executive committee and with the same rigorous certainty that candidates were free of decency and kindness. His problem was that he hadn't given the slightest thought to whether the assholes were rotten through and through, and he hadn't actually executed any of them. But the more he told people what really happened, the more they believed he was being too modest. The more he told them he wasn't being modest, that it's what really had happened, the more they came to think he was modest to a fault. After a while they began to believe that anyone who claimed this much modesty was extremely immodest. Ballantine's fellow guests at The Cloister had reached a time in life when they had no use for people who put on airs, and he started to lose friends who considered his insistence that he had been sloppy and ineffective as a murderer to be so intolerably boastful that they couldn't stand to be around him.

Here was a man who had knocked off Asshole No. 1 by turning himself into a human arrow, who had turned Asshole No. 2 into a human mortar bomb. When this man said he didn't know exactly what happened to Asshole No. 3—he "moved out of town" and that he'd had "some kind of accident"—everybody assumed that Ballantine had done something so ingenious and brutal that he didn't want anybody to believe he was capable of such a despicable act. Ballantine had seen Asshole No. 3's name in the newspaper death notices. All the death notice said was "in an accident." Ballantine tried to take comfort from the notion that he wasn't directly responsible for the accident, except that clearly Asshole No. 3 had left town because his asshole friends were dying off. His accidental death was just as upsetting as it would have been if he had stayed around and ended up getting killed accidentally as a result of Ballantine's effort to murder him.

Ballantine's fellow guests' opinions didn't bother him, though. He had long since given up trying to impress anybody, which, of course, impressed everybody in The Cloister more than anything.

At least he was busy. But in time he began to ask himself whether there might be more to life than keeping busy. Sometimes he even wondered whether there was more to life than life. As far as the life he was leading went, Ballantine sometimes got the feeling he'd had it.

"Enough is enough," he said to Mt. Rushmore.

"What if it isn't?" Mt. Rushmore asked.

"Not that I particularly want to be dead." Ballantine flung a hand dismissively around the Concourse, where they were keeping an eye on the front door because they thought they might surprise that snoopy policeman Borofsky sneaking in to take them by surprise.

"But I don't think this is all that attractive an alternative."

"You don't care if you're alive or not?"

Ballantine leaned back and scratched his tummy. "I'm not afraid, if that's what you mean."

"Who said anything about being afraid?"

"All I said was enough is enough."

"All I said was what if it isn't?"

There were guests who wanted to live forever and worked actively toward it. The ethereal return of Screaming Maureen's late husband gave them hope, although whether there needed to be more to an afterlife than sex and vindictiveness prompted considerable discussion. Among the guests were a few who always said the smartest thing they ever did was arrange to send their remains to Colorado to be immersed in liquid nitrogen.

They said that by the time somebody figured out how to thaw them out, somebody would figure out how to rejuvenate what was brought back to life.

"What if nobody does?" said Fastrack.

"What if nobody does what?" asked Ballantine.

"You'll see," said Fastrack.

Just because nobody talked about it didn't mean nobody knew the funeral homes had been making it coming and going for years. If the deceased hadn't actually decided not to become an organ donor—and how many people signed cards saying "Do *not* donate any of the organs herein contained"?—why should the funeral homes not recycle like everybody else? Is a grieving family going to know whether the corpse still has a kidney or two? If they weren't specifically designated as donations, what was to prevent funeral homes from selling the organs to the highest bidder?

Every stiff under the age of forty that didn't have a signed organ-donor agreement was what funeral directors call "an empty" since that's what it amounted to by the time of burial. Only enough remains remained to be put on display. It occurred to Fastrack that these empties could be valuable as replacement exteriors for individuals who had their brains and innards fast-frozen when they died, but would like something younger in the way of appearance and physique when they get around to being thawed out. Certainly they should be as valuable as their former contents were as innards.

"Nobody gets planted with the lid open," Fastrack said.

"You crazy?" said Speed. "Everybody I see has the lid open."

"I said 'gets planted.' At the viewing, the lid is open. Sometimes at the eulogizing. But never at the planting. Who knows what could happen in between?"

The first salvo in Fastrack's public awareness campaign was provocative. The public awareness campaign for organ donations was based on tragic stories that triggered humane responses of generosity and altruism. Fastrack's public awareness campaign for carcasses was based on the profit motive. "Having received payment, and by the terms agreed upon, I will provide what remaining remains remain to etc., etc." Signed. Witnessed. Dated. Ironclad.

When the funeral homes complained that Fastrack was cutting them out of the loop, Fastrack advised them to get a grip. Did not a great number of Grade A organs end up in their shops that weren't committed to future use despite an intense campaign to get those organs donated? Fastrack was prepared to offer a similar arrangement. He would pay top prices for prime empties that hadn't already sold their remaining remains to him ahead of their departure. It would be a simple matter of sliding them discreetly out of the coffins before consigning them to the earth, or the fire. The funeral homes had to admit this wasn't such a bad deal after all.

It was a better deal for the executive committee at The Cloister, which turned it over to a subcommittee headed by John Dillinger. Living individuals who saw an opportunity to make a quick buck by selling their bodies, but who hadn't read the contract carefully, were reminded by nice old people who visited them in their homes or workplaces that their end of the bargain had to be fulfilled by age forty, and that the date was approaching. And if they failed to deliver on or before the due date, the nice old people would return and collect either the original payment, plus interest, or the non-complying client, now a corpse, by quick and painless lethal injection.

Mt. Rushmore argued that the candidates the executive committee approved for execution had been thoroughly vetted and had, to everyone's satisfaction, proved that it was better for the whole world if they were murdered. What Fastrack and John Dillinger were proposing was killing people to order.

But for good business reasons, said John Dillinger. The stiffs will be obliged to become stiffs because they failed to comply with the terms of the contract they signed, and for which they had been very well paid.

"But we're not in business," said Sister Bernice.

"We can use this business to finance the business we're not in."

"That's an interesting point," said Sister Bernice.

"Is it?" said Mt. Rushmore.

"Yes," said John Dillinger.

What The Cloister's executive committee gained, besides a nice little income, was an improved injectable lethal substance and a productive new tactic. It was a variation on a method that children used instinctively, but that had never been attempted by the elderly. While even half a dozen of The Cloister's guests were no match for the average citizen under forty, thirty of them could overwhelm anybody for the length of time necessary to jam a hypodermic needle into a thigh. Witnesses were invariably at a loss to know exactly what had happened since the incident seemed inexplicable.

The problem was supply and demand. The number of wackos who had arranged to have their bodies frozen and then fell for what Fastrack was selling was microscopic compared to the enormous inventory John Dillinger was building.

"What do you think a person might do," he would ask, as if considering an obscure theory, "if he happened to have 165 top-quality human carcasses on hand?"

"Holy shit!" said Mt. Rushmore.

"Where the hell do you keep 165 stiffs?" asked Ballantine, who had never realized the scope of Fastrack's operation.

"I am just discussing this as a matter of intellectual interest," Fastrack would say. "Perhaps in a freezer unit at the wholesale food terminal."

"Hey! That's where I had my business." Ballantine sounded pleased. It wasn't every day he got a chance to discuss his previous career.

Mt. Rushmore said, "You mean, down there, somebody's got a couple hundred sides of beef in one unit, and somebody's got a couple hundred slaughtered pigs in the next unit. And you've got 165 stiffs in the unit next to theirs?"

"They have some very big units," Ballantine said.

"Holy shit!"

Then a thought occurred to Ballantine, based on experience. "What about shelf life?"

"That could present a problem," Fastrack said. "If they weren't selling like hotcakes."

"Or there's a power failure," said Mt. Rushmore.

"It could be you're a little ahead of the curve," Ballantine said. "Do you suppose there might be some highly civilized cannibals somewhere who have put the old life behind them but still long for their traditional diet?"

"Oh for Christ's sake," said Mt. Rushmore.

"On feast days, maybe," Ballantine suggested.

e i g h t e e n

MINIMUM MAX DIDN'T WANT to be a Messiah. Messiahs came to bad ends. "Name one," Minimum Max would say to his flock, "who didn't."

When he added things up, though, he couldn't avoid coming to the obvious conclusion—they added up to being a Messiah. He had been celibate his whole life. It hadn't been intentional. It just worked out that way. But why else would it have worked out that way?

He'd had a colostomy. His asshole was never fouled by earthly corruption.

He didn't have any disciples, but then he hadn't performed any miracles, and miracles were what brought disciples through the door. Max's current flock wasn't disciple material. You could light the fuse on a miracle and drop it down the front of their pants and they wouldn't notice, let alone be transformed.

Minimum Max didn't believe in a supreme being. He didn't *not* believe either. He had never given it any thought one way or the other until it occurred to him that he might be a Messiah.

Nobody in The Cloister knew questions like this were on Max's mind, but then nobody knew that anything was on Max's mind. Nobody could recall hearing him say anything. They would have been astonished to discover that what was on his mind was the messianic founding of the Church of the Second Coming of

Christ, Assassin. He had kept it to himself because the timing wasn't right.

It was all on tape, though.

"Everything," Borofsky said.

"It's news to me," said Mt. Rushmore.

"Times, dates, everything." Borofsky was emptying out the two plastic shopping bags he carried into the Evening Cookie Club. His arrival had caused a muted sensation. By now everybody was getting used to seeing him around, although when and where were unpredictable. He put a crimp in conversation. Mt. Rushmore said, "Sometimes when he's been here, it's two weeks before I can even fart."

"You knew about him thinking he was the Messiah?" Borofsky assembled the stuff into two piles—videocassettes and transcripts of the videotapes.

"Not until he rowed out there and told us he was going to walk on the water," Ballantine said.

"There are a lot of people in here you never know what they're thinking. All the gagas," Mt. Rushmore said patiently. Not so patiently that he might offend their visitor by intimating he was bone stupid, but patiently as if working it out in his own mind and wanting to be sure he got it right. "Sometimes you get the feeling with some of them that they're trying really hard to tell you what they're thinking, but it makes no sense. Then there are some guests whose every thought is fresh as a new-blooming flower. Yours truly, for example. But sometimes, even when I know exactly what I'm thinking, I might start telling it to you and, right here in the middle of two words, I'll forget either what I had been thinking, or what I was going to tell you about what I'd been thinking. Now between these extremes are many speeds and variations. Ballantine here is what I would call relatively high functioning."

Ballantine smiled gravely.

"And then there are folks like Minimum Max. Since you don't know what the fuck they're going on about half the time, unless it is of the utmost importance—for instance, he's trying to tell you your shoes are on fire—you tune him out. Not gaga, but semi. So when he says he's going to walk on the water—if he did actually say it beforehand and I don't recall that he did—most of us wouldn't pay too much attention. As for ending up there to see him do it—"

"We thought we were going for an outing on one of the casino boats," Ballantine said. "That's why there was such a good turnout."

"Bait and switch," said Mt. Rushmore. "The old bait and switch. You telling us you don't have crazy people working at the police department? Nobody, you see him coming, you don't say, oh-oh, here comes fucking whatsisname, I'm out of here?"

Borofsky held up both hands. "When I say it's all on tape, there's no actual times or dates or anything. There's just some very interesting things. I thought you'd be interested. Mostly what he says is gibberish. But then," and he started flipping through the pile of stapled transcripts, "look at this."

It was just as Minimum Max had expected. The miracle would change everything. All kinds of people would pay attention to him. And all because, for the first time,

Minimum Max felt love. That's not how Mt. Rushmore eventually summed it up on "News & Views Roundup," though. He summed it up this way: "All his life Minimum Max had been misunderstood and didn't know it."

"What was that supposed to mean?" Ballantine asked after the show.

Mt. Rushmore glared indignantly down his nose. "There you go, shooting the messenger."

"I'm not shooting the messenger. I just wondered what it meant."

"They always shoot the messenger," said Mt. Rushmore, turning on his heel and walking away.

As far as Minimum Max knew, he was the only Messiah currently in operation, and certainly the only one in The Cloister. If there were others, they never let on after he received the sign from on high to start going around dressed like one. The sign hadn't been anything obvious like flaming letters appearing on the mirror while he was shaving. It was more like an awareness. All of a sudden everything added up.

He started attending the regular services in The Cloister so he could see what other religions did to attract a flock. One thing he noticed was that at the end everybody got up and left, except for a handful of gagas who hadn't wandered off on their own during the service. These were docile souls accustomed to being led, so they stayed where they had been put. One day whoever was supposed to take one particular bunch of leftovers away failed to show up. Minimum Max, who had never spoken before an audience in his life, decided this would be an ideal opportunity. He sidled to the front, turned to face them, took a deep breath, spread his arms, and let fly.

"Friends!"

But it came out so low-keyed that nobody heard it. Even Minimum Max hardly heard it.

He took another deep breath. He spread his arms wider. He hollered "Dear friends!" so loud that the gagas twittered and gibbered.

He waved his arms around. They stared at him, open-mouthed. Minimum Max felt something like electricity begin at his toes and vibrate up his legs and into his belly, his lungs—his heart! They weren't turning away the way everybody else did when Minimum Max showed up. Their attention was intense. It warmed Minimum Max like the July sun. The attendant who finally arrived to lead them away saw that Minimum Max had them all under control and went off on other business.

As the weeks passed, it became customary for Minimum Max to slip in at the end of one service or another. When there were two or three on at the same time, he arranged with the various clergy to deposit their leftovers at a prearranged site. The staff was happy. They never knew what to do with gagas. They even rounded up loose gagas who were trailing here and there and led them to where Minimum Max was preaching and locked the door so they couldn't wander off again. This created a heightened atmosphere that Minimum Max found stimulating: worshippers walking into walls, defecating on the carpet. Ululating cries would multiply as dozens of members of his flock shuffled in circles. Minimum Max could feel that something beyond his own person, beyond even his own soul, was getting everybody stoked up.

In return for the love the gagas shone on him, Minimum Max felt the need to give, but what did he have to offer beyond his own love? He could let them in on the news that he was a Messiah. But they wouldn't know what he was talking about, and nobody else would believe him unless he could perform a miracle to show he had the credentials.

But what kind of miracle? He worked up his nerve and took a poll in the dining room. What was the biggest miracle in history? A lot of guests said Jonah and the whale. One whole table couldn't remember any miracles at all until a woman said, "Moses pissing on that rock," and everybody else at the table agreed. Word got around, and for several days, whenever Minimum Max showed up with his clipboard and asked, the answer he got was Moses pissing on that rock, or Moses pissing on something else—that mountain, the walls of Jericho, Noah's Ark.

Minimum Max narrowed the question to miracles by Jesus. "The wedding at Cana," said one woman. She sighed. "It was so lovely."

Minimum Max had never heard of it. "What happened there?"

"He pissed in the wine."

There was the old standby about the loaves and fishes. Except food seemed to appear out of nowhere in the dining room three times a day, so a catering miracle wouldn't be much of a grabber. Then it came to him.

How had Jesus got the fishes in the first place? Why, he'd walked out and grabbed them. No non-miraculous person would be able to pull off something like that.

Minimum Max took the subway to the Y, put on a bathing suit, and stood by the side of the pool, psyching himself up. No—honing his faith to a razor's edge. Carefully he placed one foot on the surface of the water, but it went right through. His faith wasn't as solid as it needed to be; he had doubt in his heart, and that made his foot sink. He needed to believe. He retreated to the wall and stared at the water.

People started to look at him, but the Y was the Y and nobody looked at anybody too hard for fear of establishing eye contact, which could lead to more trouble than you maybe were looking for unless you came there with the express purpose of establishing eye contact. The lifeguard wondered if the old fuck was going to have a seizure or something. A rasping, hollow inhale, a rushing, wheezing exhale, a gasped "I believe!" Over and over. "I believe! I believe! I believe! I believe!" Until Minimum Max believed!

The instant he did he ran toward the pool.

Somebody yelled. People turned. They saw an old fuck, his legs pumping as if he were on a bicycle, sail out over the water's surface—and drop like a rock. The lifeguards hauled him out, stood him up, and told him he had violated the most fundamental of all Y rules. No running by the pool. Because it wasn't until he began to sink that he had given serious thought to the fact that he didn't know how to swim, Max couldn't calm down enough to explain. When they threw him out, he stood in the street shaking and clutching a towel around his waist. He had done it! For that instant when his belief had been most profound, he had actually felt the water supporting him. He had skittered! And, with the aftertaste of chlorine in his throat and in his nostrils, he realized that if the water had been pure, inviolate water, it wouldn't have given way. He would have skittered the width of the pool. And what had happened? He had been expelled from the Y, expelled because of his beliefs. Because of his messianic gifts. It was the first time he had felt the scourge of persecution, and it made him weep with joy.

The founder of the Church of the Second Coming of Christ, Assassin, was unique in two ways, although he didn't know it. He was the first Messiah to actually start a church. And he was the first one to create his own gospel. Until the Gospel of Max, gospels were about the Messiah, not by the Messiah. But then Max didn't actually write his—he videotaped it, creating a true and lasting record of his preachings. Like the Christian Messiah, Minimum Max was deeply involved in the concept of everlasting life. Unlike that Messiah, he had never brought a dead person back to life, but doing that didn't interest him particularly. What Max had was the gift of bringing on sudden death. Gift? Not gift, talent. Not even talent. What Max had was the power!

All he had to do was blink and some wicked person would die. But it would look natural. In the case of Mrs. Marilyn Merrick, it looked as if she had been shot by Mr. Murray Merrick. The chairman of the Big One Confederated Bank? Struck by lightning? That could have been a fluke. When the explosive charges were found sown the length and breadth of the fourteenth tee, his flock would realize that it was actually the work of Max.

And so it came to pass.

And so it was recorded by Minimum Max's evangelist, Sony.

Five clear cases, each highlighted with yellow marker by Borofsky, the latest being Reeta Bishop, a fashion designer and child molester with a penchant for videotapes herself. Videos of herself molesting children while wearing her latest creations—precisely targeted advertising for a very exclusive clientele. Max had the location—the Battersea Ballroom. And the time—just as she opened her mouth to thank everyone for coming to celebrate her sixtieth birthday. And the means—a stabbing. Stabbings were rare, but it had been a special request by the nominator after Bishop had been approved by the full committee. And what Borofsky emphasized was that, according to the date on the tape, Max had recorded it four days before it occurred.

"What do you think about that?" asked Borofsky.

"Son of a bitch," said Mt. Rushmore.

Borofsky looked as if he'd been expecting a different response.

Mt. Rushmore frowned. "Son of a bitch."

It was easy enough to understand why Max might have confused cause and effect. He had attended all the executive committee meetings and followed all the deliberations. How bad was such and such a person? Did the candidate have any redeeming qualities?

Messiahs had always been known as redeemers, and now here he was, able to do a little redeeming himself. If the person had redeeming qualities, Minimum Max could cash them in like airline points. What the committee members, who came away from the meetings thinking it was their votes that had swung things one way or the other, didn't realize was that the shot had really been called by Max. He regarded the committee's vote as a mere expression of opinion, which he, being a democratically inclined Messiah, would invariably accept. He would signal his acceptance by blinking twice rapidly. And his will was done.

It wasn't quite that clear in the transcripts. Ballantine and Mt. Rushmore agreed with Borofsky that there was a lot of gibberish. All you got was the drift. Uncomfortably, though, the drift was always in the right direction and in advance of events.

The turnout was enormous, but Minimum Max had used a clever ploy. "Outing, May 27. *Not to Total!*" Somehow the rumour spread that a casino boat had been laid on for an afternoon's cruise, and so many people signed up that extra buses had to be chartered. When they got to the waterfront there was a great deal of confusion. Where was the casino boat? The guests stumbled off the buses and milled around asking what the hell was going on. They couldn't see a boat of any kind. But there was one. It was behind a breakwater wall at the foot of a launch ramp fishermen used.

They discovered the boat was there when Minimum Max splashed around the end of the wall and up the ramp. He was wearing what looked like a full length white nightgown. Taped on it, over his heart—although they couldn't see this until he got right up close—was a picture of a heart with flames rising out the top that he must have clipped from some religious magazine.

"Anybody know about motors?"

Everybody was thunderstruck, but ten or twelve men went to the edge of the breakwater as Minimum Max climbed into an aluminum boat and pointed at an outboard. "It won't start."

"There's no fucking gas tank."

"What?"

"There's no gas tank!"

"It needs a gas tank? Then I'll use this." There was an oar in the bottom of the boat, grey and scraped and chewed at the end.

"What the fuck's going on?"

"I'm going to walk on the water," Minimum Max said, pushing against the breakwall with his oar and pointing the boat's nose into the chop.

For fifteen minutes he paddled, awkwardly, precariously, away from the shore. As word spread that Minimum Max was going to walk on the water, guests crowded closer to the shore, hunched against the breeze and wondering if they'd lost their collective mind. It was May and they had begun to shiver as soon as they climbed down from the buses. It had never occurred to them that an outing might involve being outside.

The waves slapping at Max's boat filled his eyes with spray. When at last he stood up, everybody could see that he was having trouble keeping his balance. He sat down quickly. He gripped the sides to steady himself, but he couldn't. He appeared uncertain as to how to proceed. He seemed to be contemplating the discovery that it would be extremely tricky to step out of a boat and on to the water's surface even if they both remained perfectly still. After some time, he twisted around so he could dangle his feet over the side. He wriggled along until he was sitting on the rusted oarlock, which caused the boat to tip sharply and plop him into the water, where he disappeared from sight.

"Jesus Christ!"

"Holy shit!"

Somebody with a cellphone called 911.

While they waited for help to arrive, there was nothing to do but stare at the empty boat bobbing where Minimum Max had disappeared. After about twenty minutes a police boat roared up, by which time most guests had shuffled back into the buses, the doors had been closed, and the heat turned on. Many of the gagas had drifted off here and there as the drama unfolded. Had Minimum Max been able to preach the following Sunday, a quarter of his regular congregation would have been absent. When the police scuba divers who had jumped in hadn't reappeared after fifteen minutes, the buses drove away.

Borofsky fixed Mt. Rushmore with a narrow gaze. "What do you mean when you say 'Son of a bitch'?"

"I mean—" said Mt. Rushmore.

He clutched Ballantine's shoulder. His voice filled with horror and astonishment. "Minimum Max was a murderer!"

Ballantine's jaw dropped. He closed his mouth. He swallowed. His jaw dropped again.

"A mass murderer," said Mt. Rushmore.

"You think?" was all Ballantine could choke out.

"Fuckin' right." Mt. Rushmore shook a finger at Borofsky. "Fuckin' right."

"Killed all those—" Ballantine was trying to get his voice back up from his lungs.

"Five of them," said Mt. Rushmore.

"Five—"

"Killed five people." Mt. Rushmore nodded with a profound certainty.

"You are out of your fucking minds," Borofsky said.

"Killed them. Then took us all down to the water to—"

"—watch him kill himself. Commit suicide." Ballantine was trying not to shout out at the madness of it all.

"Guilt," boomed Mt. Rushmore, tapping Borofsky on the breastbone. "Guilty conscience. Got him in the end."

Borofsky stood and jammed his tapes and documents back into the plastic shopping bags.

Ballantine was trying to keep from falling over. Laughter was boiling up from deep in his intestines and threatening to explode. He didn't dare look at Borofsky. He didn't dare look at Mt. Rushmore.

"You fuckers," Borofsky said. "You *fuckers!*"

"I feel bad about that," Mt. Rushmore said as they watched Borofsky and his shopping bags disappear through the door.

"Not knowing Minimum Max was so nuts?" Ballantine asked.

"Blaming a poor dead guy for what's been going on."

Ballantine nodded. "You're right. It was a dreadful thing to do."

"It was." Mt. Rushmore looked wistful. "But sometimes awful things have got to be done. In fact, the minute you kick off, I'm turning you in."

Ballantine was gathering his strength to get out of the chair. "I don't believe you."

"Believe me. I'm doing it."

"Why?"

"For the reward."

n i n t e e n

MILES G. CONCANNON WAS one rich son of a
bitch. "Says so right here." Sister Bernice pointed to the
accolade on the cover of *Business Time*, when the magazine named him Entrepreneur of the Millennium. "A
Five-Star Son of a Bitch" is what it said.

"When charity went global," Sister Bernice said, "he
cornered the market." Of every dollar donated to a worthy cause on the planet, seventeen cents went directly
into Miles Concannon's treasury. It didn't matter what
the worthy cause was. Anti-abortion was as worthy as
abortion on demand as long as he got seventeen cents of
every dollar donated to fight abortion or defend the
right of women to decide what happened to their bodies.

Concannon didn't interfere with anybody's freedom to
choose a beneficial organization. It was a free world. The
minute a new disease was discovered, Concannon's agents
were tying up the long-term charitable rights. Even some
diseases widely considered to have died out were kept in
an active file by Concannon. Bubonic plague was one of
these because it was so highly regarded as a potential bac-
teriological weapon that it might easily get spread around
the world again, prompting concerned individuals to seek
financial assistance from the public to combat it.

Sister Bernice mimicked the advertisements. "The
New United Way is the Miles Concannon Way." One
donation was all it took. It salved your conscience.

Governments around the world, led by people who received most of their financing from Miles Concannon, made it mandatory, based on income. Your contribution was divvied up among every cause, minus seventeen percent that went to Concannon and fifty-three percent to administer the Concannon operation and cover the costs of examining claims of entitlement put forward by charities seeking a cut of the remaining thirty percent.

"Now," said Sister Bernice, "he has a new angle." She turned to her flip chart and tried to think of what to write. Finally she wrote "Ficky-fick" and underlined it. "What we have now is him coming here to introduce his scheme to privatize it."

Black-Eyed Susan sounded uncertain. "Does that say ficky-fick?"

"Okay." Sister Bernice regrouped. "When I say privatize it, I mean charge for it."

Black-Eyed Susan sounded just as uncertain. "Charge for ficky-fick?"

"So governments can collect tax on it," said Sister Bernice.

The other members of the executive committee sat in wide-eyed silence, as if they had just been run over by rubber chickens.

At last Mt. Rushmore spoke. "When you say ficky-fick—"

"You don't mean—" Black-Eyed Susan began.

"Yes, I do," said Sister Bernice.

Speed couldn't stand it anymore. "Why do you keep saying ficky-fick? Why don't you come right out and use the real words?"

"What real words?"

"Sexual intercourse."

"Eeeew!" shrilled a knitting lady.

"Dirty, dirty, dirty, dirty," all the knitting ladies shrilled.

"Way to go, Speed," Mt. Rushmore glowered.

"What the fuck is going on here?" Speed was truly bewildered.

"Oh," sighed Sister Bernice, "we're just trying to conduct a briefing in a civilized fashion and you come along and make it X-rated."

"Dirty, dirty, dirty, dirty," said the knitting ladies.

"What about," Ballantine said, "when you don't, you know, ficky-fick?"

"Yup! And," Sister Bernice turned back to her flip chart and wrote a list.

People cried, "That's insane! What about—"

"Yup," said Sister Bernice.

"Yup, what?"

"Yup, everything. You name it, it's going to cost."

"What if I"—the knitting lady had her eyes squeezed shut as if she was trying to work this all out—"I, or somebody, you know, faked it?"

"You play," said Sister Bernice, "you pay."

A computer chip would be embedded under the skin of every person on earth. Every time anyone experienced sexual stimulation, voluntarily or involuntarily, a signal would be sent to a satellite that would record the data, describe the nature and duration, calculate the bill, and send it out. When payment was received, seventeen percent would go into Miles Concannon's personal treasury, fifty-three percent would go toward administration, and the remaining thirty percent would go to the government in whose jurisdiction the stimulation had occurred.

The primary Concannon selling point was that the most difficult problems, from crime to wars to pollution to overcrowding, were caused by people, and this was the fairest way to make the people pay—by taxing them at the source.

Miles Concannon, for a reasonable fee, would provide the subcutaneous computer chips, insertion teams and equipment, the satellites and sexual-stimulation scanners, as well as the computer program and infrastructure needed to send out the monthly bills. And anyone who failed to pay on time would never be stimulated sexually again. He guaranteed that.

No one was allowed within 500 metres of the hotel where Concannon was going to unveil his scheme without submitting to a cavity search. Once invitation holders reached the hotel entrance, they were given back their clothes, which had been fumigated, x-rayed, analyzed by DNA sniffing machines to establish the identity of the wearer, and pissed on by Concannon Security Service dogs that could then track down and, if necessary, rip the throat out of whoever had them on.

The dinner crowd in the grand ballroom included representatives of every level of government and ambassadors from seventy-five United Nations countries eager to see the Concannon system introduced so they could come to grips with the incredible obstacles people presented to the smooth operations of their governments. Arab oil sheiks, Nobel prize winners, the corporate aristocracy of the age, and fifteen top clerics were there to bask in the glory of the greatest living business mind of the age and to see how they could most profitably incorporate his scheme into their financial institutions.

Halfway through the first course, Mt. Rushmore appeared at the security barrier under enormous banners emblazoned with "Make the People's Seed Pay for the People's Need." It took him some time to get anybody's attention even though he was wearing a tall papier-mâché hat shaped like an erect penis. When he finally did, he said, "I'm in charge of the entertainment."

The security agent looked blank.

"We're the Dickhead Dancers." Mt. Rushmore pointed behind him to the two busloads of guests from The Cloister, all wearing similar hats.

The security agent looked blank.

"I'm the choreographer."

The security agent spoke into a microphone on his lapel. "This is S-52." Mt. Rushmore could see his beautiful plan about to collapse. "Yeah, base," the security agent said, tapping his earphone. "There's fuck all doing out here. How about I go on my break?" Mt. Rushmore watched him walk away, then gave the buses a thumbs-up.

The lights dimmed. A single spotlight picked out Mt. Rushmore on a riser behind the head table. There was a smattering of awkward laughter.

"Good evening, ladies and gentlemen. We want to welcome you to our wonderful, wonderful city. On this magnificent occasion—to set the mood—I'm honoured to present one of the foremost ensembles of its kind, the Dickhead Dancers."

More awkward laughter. A rustle of applause.

The surge of adrenalin almost lifted Mt. Rushmore off his feet. He hadn't felt anything like it since the choreographic vision had come to him during the Total riot.

He began to snap his fingers. Snap, snap, snap, snap— a regular beat. It was picked up here and there along the walls. Snap, snap, snap, snap. The snapping got louder as people emerged from the shadows wearing erect penises on their heads. They moved haltingly, shuffling to the beat. Snap, snap, snap, snap, louder still and more insistent. More and more of them flooded into the room from the service entrances.

"Mr. Concannon." Mt. Rushmore's voice had taken on a harsh edge. "This is one killer dance you are about to see."

Undulating and nodding, the penis people filled the spaces between the tables. There was something almost scrotal about the aged faces under them. From time to time one would rise on tiptoes and grunt, then rise and grunt again, and again, faster and faster. When the risings and grunts reached a peak, audience members nearby laughed exuberantly and cheered. An orgasm! How delightful! And more delightful still—another Jimmy McDrool triumph— the penises spouted dollar bills with Miles Concannon's face on them. "Brilliant!" people cried. "Bravo!"

As the hilarity grew, Concannon demanded to know what the fuck was going on. Why had nobody told him about this stupid entertainment thing? Since none of his aides wanted to let on that they hadn't known about it either, they said it had been planned as a surprise for him by the mayor to show the gratitude of all the mayors of all the cities who would reap the harvest that

Concannon was going to sow for them. As the aides reminded Concannon what a cornball huckster the mayor was, the mayor burst into their huddle. He had to hand it to Concannon, he said. He knew when he was in the presence of genius. He wished he had the imagination and audacity to come up with a stunt like the Dickhead Dancers.

Concannon scowled at the mayor. He scowled at his aides. He scowled at the room. The dancing penises had concentrated in a semicircle in front of the head table and were moving in a synchronized, gimpy rhythm that sent an unpleasant chill between Concannon's shoulder blades.

All together they rose to tiptoe and then shrank down. All together they grunted. Rose, shrank. Grunted. Picking up the pace. Up and down, up and down. Grunt, grunt, grunt, grunt! Faster and faster until their grunting became a gasping roar and thousands of Concannon dollar bills shot from the tips of their headgear, filling the air like confetti.

"Fuck me," Concannon said. The sound of his own voice seemed to unnerve him. For the first time in his life he appeared to be at a loss. Elbowing the mayor aside, two aides took hold of him as he was about to faint. One of them pulled an automatic pistol from a shoulder holster, the other shouted something into his lapel. A dozen security agents materialized around Concannon and pushed through a door at the back of the room. They rushed for the service elevators. Hobbling behind came The Cloister's performers, grunting rhythmically.

From the roof of a building a block and a half away, Banana saw the knot of people burst from a doorway on the roof of the hotel and move toward the Concannon helicopter. Banana's view was magnified sixty times by the digital video camera hooked to the laptop computer he was watching. The camera was attached to the motorized sight on the Modox WB99/SU—SU for Sniper Unit—that he and Speed had acquired over the Internet from an arms dealer in Damascus who was keen to receive feedback since it was a prototype in development by an innovative manufacturer in West Virginia and not yet available to the guerrilla forces that opposed national armies all around the world.

The idea behind the Modox WB99 was that a weapon easily identifiable as a weapon was a liability for insurgency operations in urban environments. Guns originally looked like guns because form followed function. They continued to look like guns because of the immense satisfaction they gave to those who possessed them. There was something enabling in simply feeling the weight in one's hands, the way the grips and stocks became a natural extension of one's physical self. But a gun where no gun was supposed to be was often alarming.

None of this was necessary, of course, other than sensually and esthetically. A gun could just as effectively be shaped like a volleyball. Or, like Banana's Modox WB99, a compact nylon container with a telescoping handle and little wheels—an airline carry-on wheelie bag. Set up its tripod, place the bag on top, snap on the remote camera-aimer, run a wire to the computer-mouse trigger. The cursor on the screen Banana was watching was a bull's eye. As Concannon moved across the roof of the hotel, Banana moved the mouse, keeping the bull's eye on his chest.

The old make-the-quarry-take-flight-then-ambush-the-son-of-a-bitch dodge.

Well before the final executive committee briefing, Mt. Rushmore realized there was going to be a problem.

"They're going to give you a hard time," he said.

Ballantine exhaled slowly. He knew.

"Banana's losing it," Mt. Rushmore said.

"We're all losing it."

Mt. Rushmore's shoulders slumped. "He could fuck it up."

Ballantine thought about this for a couple of seconds. "He could," he said. "So what?"

"So what?" How the hell could anybody say "So what?" But before Mt. Rushmore could say anything, Ballantine took him by the arm. "What difference does it make?"

And for all his desire to let his rage blow Ballantine to fucking kingdom come, he couldn't. Because he couldn't, for the life of him, think what difference it would make.

"He'll never pull it off!" Chardonnay declared, getting to her feet and speaking to the first order of business.

Banana looked crestfallen.

"Now, now, now," said Sister Bernice.

"Now, now, nothing," said Chardonnay. "I've been paying pretty close attention, and he is losing it." Banana stared forlornly at his knees.

Ballantine was working up the energy to wade in when Mt. Rushmore surprised him. "It's all computerized," Mt. Rushmore said. "It doesn't call for anything superhuman."

"It's anything human I'm worried about." Chardonnay tapped her front teeth with an angry thumbnail. "Listen, I'm not here to insult him. I'm just saying, why take chances? This job's worth doing, so why not use the best person?"

"Maybe he is the best person," said Mt. Rushmore.

"Yeah, sure."

"And maybe he most deserves the chance."

"What's that supposed to mean?" Nobody had ever heard Chardonnay sound more prosecutorial.

"It means, it was his idea."

"The setup." Now Sister Bernice was getting into the act. "The setup, the weapon. The whole schmear. It was all his doing."

"What about what's at stake?"

Sister Bernice thought a minute. "Maybe that's what's at stake."

Despite all this fine talk in Banana's defence, Ballantine wasn't completely sure anything should be at stake. He thought back to the conversation he'd had with Speed who admitted Miles G. Concannon's availability as a target of opportunity wasn't entirely coincidental.

"Me and John Dillinger. We're trying to make up for the Abu Badali thing." He seemed to be seeking Ballantine's blessing. "For going off on our own? For going beyond public transit?"

"So somehow or other you contrived—"

"Through the mayor's office." Speed was obviously very proud.

"The mayor's office?"

"We got good people there."

"You arranged"—Ballantine was working through this one step at a time—"for Concannon to come here to make his big announcement."

"Where we can get to him on the bus."

"I think you're missing the point," Ballantine had said.

"What's the point?" Speed had replied.

Good point.

Banana kept the cursor on Concannon's chest and the Modox WB99 whirred softly as it made minute adjustments to its aim. The plan was simple. Have Concannon driven into your sights. Knock him off. But the inferno in Banana's heart was the hellfire of showbiz, and he didn't want simple. He wanted spectacle. He wanted to lay 'em in the aisles. So there was more to the plan he'd sold the committee than bringing death to the nastiest man on earth. It went to the roots of Banana's being. It went to the roots of comedy. That was why it was crucial that Concannon be precisely aligned with the chopper's bulbous fuel tank when the Modox WB99 was fired.

When he was, the round—titanium coated with magnesium—would punch a hole through the human target and penetrate the fuel tank. As oily flames consumed everyone and everything on the roof and then floated into the sky, a seething ball scalding the city with its pulsing orange glare, Banana would be ready.

"Fuck you and the helicopter you came on," he would shout.

God would fall down laughing.

Banana was almost falling down laughing. His insides were jumping in mirthful anticipation. This exaggerated the tremor in Banana's hand. Beyond that, there were involuntary twitches, mini-spasms. Of the wrist. Of the fingers. In a thousandth of a second, the bull's eye cursor dipped at precisely the instant Concannon moved around the chopper's tail rotor and strode toward the entry hatch.

Banana corrected quickly, almost subconsciously, but as he did, the index finger that had been resting lightly on the left mouse button twitched, and he shot Miles Concannon in the nuts.

t w e n t y

BANANA REFUSED TO COME OUT of his room. Through the door he shouted to Ballantine that he was upset about blowing the execution and not getting a chance to yell "Fuck you and the helicopter you came on."

"Why did you want to yell that?" Ballantine shouted back.

"You don't get it?"

"What?"

"The joke?"

Ballantine didn't know what to shout.

"I had it all worked out!" Banana shouted.

The executive committee meeting that night was strained. It was the first time they'd ended up with a candidate who wasn't dead, but wounded and on the loose. They didn't know the nature of Concannon's injury, though; the public hadn't been informed. Concannon had been flown aboard the Concannon Way helicopter, which, despite a tire flattened by Banana's round, was still airworthy, to the biggest hospital in the city, where the surgical team that travelled with him commandeered an operating room only to discover it was too late. But it wasn't until reporters from a British Sunday tabloid bribed the hospital cleaning staff that the public learned that when Concannon left the hospital, his nuts didn't.

It took a while longer for word to leak from the police about the peculiar weapon they found on a roof not far from where Concannon had been shot. Its esoteric qualities naturally led to the conclusion that whoever had done it had been the most sophisticated sniper on record equipped with the most sophisticated gun ever invented. And while this publicity was gratifying to the Damascus arms dealer and the West Virginia manufacturer, it led to an inescapable conclusion. Whoever shot Miles Concannon's nuts off had intended to do exactly that. It was a precision piece of work.

Banana was starving himself to death. When you are this close to the end of the line, it isn't hard to tip yourself over it. It's not as if death has to drop everything and invest a lot of effort in you.

"Hey!" Ballantine shouted through Banana's door after the full extent of Concannon's injury got out. "You came up with the funniest joke in the whole world."

"It was by accident," Banana shouted back.

If there was one person who was bound to be sympathetic when it came to the role that accident could play in the murder game, it was Ballantine. "So?"

"So it wasn't *my* joke." By this time, Banana's shout was starting to sound like a whisper.

Borofsky had an overpowering urge to get to the bottom of whatever was going on with those old folks. It was the first overpowering urge he'd had in ages. In a year he had to retire, and no cops wanted to work as his partner. They'd all seen the movies where the cop who is on the verge of retirement gets killed, but that wasn't why they didn't want to work with him. He was very old for a cop. Every other cop his age had been an ex-cop for a long time because their age plus the number of years they'd put in equalled a magic number. Borofsky had reached the magic number ten years ago, but he hadn't retired because he couldn't think what he'd do if he did. Now younger cops were entitled to assume his physical strength wasn't up to the job, his judgment wasn't as sound as it might be, his reflexes were none too sharp, and his sight and hearing no longer sufficiently acute to detect danger. But that wasn't why they didn't want to work with him.

He hated fishing. He hated golf. If he wasn't all that crazy about police work, it was something to do. He had a girlfriend who wanted him to call her "Big Red" even though she was skinny and dyed her hair. He had a wife who had developed full-blown Alzheimer's by the age of sixty and was in a private hospital in a small city two hours' drive away. His son was an insurance executive whose two great passions were fishing and golf. Sometimes his son got company tickets for a hockey game and took Borofsky. Borofsky enjoyed that, but lately there seemed to be less fighting. When he went to his son's house for dinner, his grandsons always wanted to see his gun, and Borofsky was happy to take the bullets out and let them play whatever the fuck kids play when they play with guns nowadays. This always gave his daughter-in-law a shit conniption.

He showed her the clip in his pocket. He jacked the action, pointed it at the ceiling, and pulled the trigger. Click. It turned out he had another overpowering urge. He wanted to leave a round in the chamber and blow a big fucking hole in the ceiling and deafen everybody in the room, but he controlled the urge so he'd get invited back. He would've missed the shit conniptions.

When they played a movie after dinner, he would fall asleep. When he woke up he would drive home. In the morning he would call Big Red and tell her he hadn't come by or called because he'd stayed the night at his son's house. If you were Big Red you would have thought Borofsky stayed over at his son's house a lot more times than he actually went to his son's house. One Sunday every month he drove two hours to visit his wife. He didn't know why. He started off visiting every Sunday. Then every second Sunday. Not one thing changed from visit to visit. Maybe they kept her in a fridge like the stiffs at headquarters. Every time they rolled her out, he would tell her about visiting their son and grandchildren. The whole time she would sing—sort of sing. Probably Neil Diamond. After twenty minutes or so he would feel sick to his stomach and go out on the patio, wishing he still smoked so he could have a cigarette. Then he'd say fuck it and walk around the building to the parking lot and drive the two hours home.

The next day he'd tell Big Red that he'd stayed for dinner and spent the night in a hospital guest room.

"I understand," she always said.

Nobody would work with Borofsky because Borofsky had staked out a position on police partnerships contrary to the sacred code. The contrary position Borofsky took was that if trouble came your way because your partner was behaving like an asshole, you fucked off. Of course he would tell his partner he was fucking off. His partner could then decide whether he wanted to confront the trouble he'd stirred up, or whether he would fuck off too. Once when he'd fucked off, his partner got shot in the calf. This led to an inquiry about Borofsky's failure to cover him.

"I had to go take a shit."

Then Borofsky said they should put a note in his file that he'd abandoned his partner.

And somebody said, "What good would it do? You're sixty-two years old for Christ's sake."

When Borofsky offered to put a note in his file himself and said he'd be happy to do it every time he had to go take a shit because his partner was behaving like an asshole, everybody just got up and hurried out.

twenty-one

FOR THE FIVE HUNDREDTH TIME, Sister Bernice reminded the executive committee that it wasn't a court of law. A court of law demanded proof beyond a reasonable doubt. The committee needed proof beyond all doubt. Besides, since it was also the executioner, it didn't want to take any chances.

"Why does she keep reminding us about this when she just reminded us?" whispered Digitalis, a new guest.

"She keeps forgetting," John Dillinger whispered back.

How could anything but good come from executing Hungry ("Feed Me Your Face") Pussy, the pop queen who, with her band, Vaginal Itch, advocated White supremacy, sexism, mindless loyalty to the materialistic leadership of the nation, and violence as the purest form of ego gratification? Although disc jockeys screamed it out on the radio and it was all over the huge billboards promoting her latest CD, "Line My Throat with Asbestos So I Can Swallow Flaming Cum," it pained Sister Bernice to say her name.

"Maybe they don't listen to the words. A lot of things I used to dance to, I couldn't make out anything they sang." But Digitalis's heart wasn't in what he was saying. He had never danced to anything like "Bomb Blacks," which called on the Air Force to attack the ghettoes.

But what if Hungry Pussy had a child, perhaps a daughter, or even a little niece, who was disturbed and handicapped, who had to be fed by hand, and the only talent Hungry Pussy had was blasting out nauseating tirades? It was the only way she could afford to keep the little daughter or niece alive?

"Who's," Mt. Rushmore observed, "to say what's art?"

The committee appointed advocates, and Sister Bernice warned Digitalis that he wouldn't be able to pull a fast one with an apparently resounding denunciation of Hungry Pussy that was, in fact, a cleverly disguised argument that she wasn't really entirely despicable. He might be tempted to try this to avoid upsetting his great-grandchildren who were big fans and would be desolate if she was knocked off. The committee had no stake in the matter. Every member on it would almost certainly be dead before the invective Hungry Pussy spouted would do a whole lot of damage to young people or race relations or the safety of women. The riots in London that ended with an entire subway train being set on fire and twenty-five people burned to death after a Hungry Pussy concert had to be regarded as an isolated incident. If a subway train had been set on fire in China, would anybody be this juiced up? Still, she was due in town next week for a concert.

Digitalis's condemnation took two full sessions; an hour before he was due to give his summation, he was paralyzed by a cerebral hemorrhage. The defence was eloquent and practised. Screaming Maureen had never lost a case, and since almost two weeks had passed since her husband had publicly humiliated her with his sexual experiences in the afterlife, she was in brilliant form. She concluded by pointing out what the world had gained because the committee had listened to her about a number of supposedly despicable individuals and let them—even though she was as heavy-hearted as the committee when it happened—get on with their lives.

One of the benefits was a Broadway revival of *The Sound of Music*. Mt. Rushmore said if he'd known that would happen he'd have voted for execution. He'd rather listen to Hungry Pussy than how the hills were fucking alive.

One of the knitting ladies at the back of the room was telling the others how her grandson and his partner were so proud that their tiny daughter—she was three—could sing almost every Hungry Pussy song. It was a hoot when there was company and they got her to do one of her Hungry Pussy numbers, which she wound up, as her idol did, by sticking her hands in her pants and then licking the fingers one by one.

"That's so cute!" said another knitting lady.

"Those little ones are something else," said a third.

The committee meeting had come to a halt.

"That little kid seems to get a kick out of it," observed Ballantine, who looked as if his stomach was acting up. "And it gives great-grandma there a big charge."

"You're going to say we seem to be deciding what's good for people," said Sister Bernice.

"I wasn't going to say anything."

"It's what you always say," she said. "Instead of just eliminating a candidate who is totally bad, are we going to eliminate somebody just because everybody will be better off as a result?"

"No teaching and preaching," John Dillinger said to Ballantine. "That's what you always say."

"You say we're not sitting in moral judgment!" Sister Bernice had to shout above the din of the knitting ladies.

"When did I ever say that?" Ballantine was upset.

"You say it all the time."

Anonymous e-mails began to circulate. Things like, "Flash from the *National Trash*: 'Hungry Pussy Tells All'." Mt. Rushmore read them aloud on his "News & Views Roundup."

"'When I was eleven years old,' said international hardcore pop sensation Hungry ("Feed Me Your Face") Pussy in an exclusive interview, 'my baby was born with AIDS. I put her up for adoption because I didn't want her filthifying my life. Now she is doing that thing where they get in touch with their birth mother if the birth mother is rich and an important symbol for young women everywhere. Fuck her. I don't belong to one little child. I belong to every child.'"

"Can that be right?" asked Jimmy McDrool. "She had a baby when she was eleven?"

"It says so in the *Nash Trash*," said Mt. Rushmore.

"No wonder she's messed up."

"Look here!" Mt. Rushmore pointed to the computer screen. From the *Capitol Crotch-Watcher*: "'It has been revealed through secret government documents obtained by the *Crotch-Watcher* that the precision jet-fighter flying team, the Golden Blasters, intentionally bombed the schoolyard in Charlotte, North Carolina, which resulted in the deaths of thirty-eight children. An investigation by the military ruled the tragic incident accidental.

"'Now it has been learned that it was linked directly to the May 29 air show tragedy when, during a performance at the Indiana State Fair, the only African-American pilot on the team was shot down by two fellow pilots who claimed they didn't know their F-16s were equipped with air-to-air missiles.

"'Heavy ordnance, both missiles and laser-guided bombs, have been added to some of the aircraft, apparently since the team chose Hungry ('Feed Me Your Face') Pussy's hit 'Bomb Blacks' to accompany their flying routines.'"

Mt. Rushmore looked accusingly at Ballantine.

Ballantine said, "She has sold 160 million CDs. Tell me she isn't giving somebody pleasure."

"What kind of pleasure?"

"I don't know."

Ballantine locked the door to his room and lay on the bed. "I don't care," he said to himself. "It's none of my fucking business."

It would be a mistake to call the executive committee meeting two days later deadlocked. It was just stuck. The knitting ladies didn't even bother to show up. John Dillinger said they were in the gym working on a big "Salute to Hungry Pussy" number for the upcoming "The Cloister Month in Review" show.

The next meeting was worse. "I don't think we've got a quorum," said Sister Bernice.

"What's with a quorum?" said Mt. Rushmore. "There's no set number. If it's just you, that's okay, you can have a meeting."

"We don't have a quorum," said Sister Bernice. She declared the meeting adjourned.

Mt. Rushmore didn't give a shit what the other guests thought was wonderful about Ballantine—how adept he was and bloodthirsty and wise and unassuming. Mt.

Rushmore thought the most wonderful thing was the kite story.

He always hoped he might be able to talk Ballantine into telling it one more time. "All that about the kites and you is so fucking stupid I can hardly believe it," he would say, already laughing, when he would slip up behind Ballantine, hoping to catch him off guard.

Although Ballantine didn't think it was stupid or that funny either, he'd say, "I needed something to keep busy at. That's all. Something to fill my day."

"Get to the part where the kite dragged you down the hill and across the soccer field!" Mt. Rushmore was cupping his mouth to make it look as if he had a straight face. "And everybody jumped on you and beat the shit out of you!"

Ballantine ignored him. "I was going pretty crazy in those first months after my wife was killed."

"Think of the headlines. 'Kite Flyer Disrupts Kiddies' Game—Kicked to Death by Soccer Moms.'"

"I thought maybe a hobby would help pass the time, so I—"

"Went out and bought a great big Jesus kite the size of a parachute and it dragged you right into all those fucking little…" Mt. Rushmore couldn't continue. When the choking fit passed, he tried again. "…in their fucking little soccer boots! We all do that! The minute we get home from the wife's funeral, we head for the kite store! 'Gimme a big one. Gimme the biggest fucking one you got.'"

Ballantine folded his arms and looked away. "Forget it."

"I mean big! I couldn't half wipe my ass with this piddly snot-rag of a—"

Indignation was turning Ballantine's backbone into a steel rod. "I mean it."

"Oh, please! Please!"

"Fuck you."

"I love this story," said Mt. Rushmore. "Did you really make a furrow across the soccer field with your nose before you smashed into all those little children in their fucking little soccer boots? I love it! A furrow!"

It was when he was going to the kite store, way off in a part of town he'd never spent much time in, that he saw Asshole No. 1 for the first time since the fatal incident. Only later did he realize that to reach the store, he had to get off at the same subway station the assholes got off at after scaring his wife to death. By then he'd already been back three or four times for bigger kites and more string.

"Line!" the kite store guy always said. "Not string!"

The kite store guy was one of those braided-hair, pale people who irritated Ballantine. "Health-food eaters," he called them. Ballantine had carried organic product, but only because it was fashionable in fancy neighbourhoods. He'd even eaten it to find out what it tasted like. It tasted like the regular product only more expensive. The kite store guy looked as if the only time he ever left the kite store was to go to the health-food store to buy lentils.

"Is this line?" Ballantine would ask.

"Yes."

"It looks a lot like string."

It was the third or fourth time he came out of the store that he saw Asshole No. 1. Ballantine followed him. It was a little after ten in the morning when he started and eleven that night when he quit because he was too tired to stay upright. And anyway, he'd seen enough to figure out that this was the asshole's home turf. He'd be easy enough to find when Ballantine came back the next day.

"You just changed one kind of filling in your day for another one," Mt. Rushmore said, nodding to emphasize his insight.

"Huh?"

"Killing assholes. It kept you busy."

Coming out of the kite store, the idea of killing the assholes had never occurred to him. It had never occurred to him that he'd see them again.

In a couple of weeks Ballantine had tracked down all three. It was a letdown. What was he supposed to do now, get in their faces and call them names? Then he had an idea. Why not murder them? He couldn't think of a good reason not to.

And it would give him something to do.

As much as he usually looked forward to finding Ballantine on the off chance he'd get to hear the kite story again, this time Mt. Rushmore wasn't. He didn't have a good feeling about looking for Ballantine this time. Anyway, he already knew where he was.

He banged on the door. "You in there? The meeting adjourned because there was no quorum. You ever know we needed a quorum? Hello?" He banged again. "I guess if there's no rules"—when he shouted like this, he had to catch his breath every few words—"anybody can make up any rules they want."

There was no sound from inside.

"Why not? There's no rules against it."

He pressed his ear against the door. Maybe Ballantine had kicked off.

"You seen V8? Hey! Anybody in there?"

The door jerked open.

"I haven't seen anybody," Ballantine said. He looked as if somebody had drained him and refilled him with distilled water. "I haven't been out of this fucking room for four days."

The door slammed.

"Nobody's seen her," Mt. Rushmore said.

V8 had never been on an outing before, so she wasn't at all surprised when it turned out she was the only one going and she had to ask strangers on the street for directions to the subway station.

She rode the subway for a long time without changing trains. For quite a while she sat beside an eleven-year-old girl who told her she'd just come from having an abortion and was trying to decide what to do next. After an hour or so, the girl got off. V8 decided that was a good idea, so at the next stop she got off, too. She was wearing a blue flannelette nightgown so pale from being washed that it looked white. Over that she had a blue wool coat. She had on fluffy, pale-blue bedroom slippers.

On the street, a bus was loading, so she got on. When it reached the end of its route, the driver told her that if she wasn't going to get off, she would have to pay an extra fare. Okay, she said, and gave him the money. But after a few minutes she had to find a toilet, so when the bus stopped at a plaza, she got off. When she came out of the washroom, the bus had gone.

A van with a young couple in it was pulling away from the gas pumps. "Could I get a lift?" V8 asked.

"Where to?" The man seemed friendly.

She didn't know for sure, but pointed in the direction the van seemed to be headed. "That way. Not far."

"Sure." He unlatched a door that slid open.

Before she climbed inside, V8 paused. "I don't have a gun," she said.

"Good!" He looked astonished. "Good! Come on!"

She sat very straight in the middle of the broad seat. It had grown quite dark.

The girl piped up from the driver's seat. "You said you don't have a gun?"

"Yes," said V8. "Isn't that silly?"

"No!" The girl laughed. In the dashboard glow, V8 could see the young man smiling at her. "These days, I guess nobody trusts anybody," the girl said. "It's probably good to let people know you're not, you know, armed."

V8 let her face relax. That's not what she meant. She hadn't seen her gun since she lent it to Banana, who, after shooting Miles Concannon's nuts off, had locked himself in his room for the rest of his life. To have a gun, but not to be able to put your hands on it when you needed it—wasn't that silly?

The StratoDome seated 150,000 for a football game, and 250,000 for a Christian crusade. V8 couldn't even say what part of town it was in. She just had a feeling she'd know it when she got there, and bus rides and subway rides and rides from kind folks somehow or other got her there. She didn't have a ticket, but breezed through the crush. Nobody frisked her or made her go through the metal detectors. It was now half past midnight, and Hungry ("Feed Me Your Face") Pussy was due on stage.

Everybody saw for themselves what happened after that. Hungry Pussy was into her third number when a pale figure appeared behind her. The Hungry Pussy Tour Organization tape of the performance had a wide shot of the stage with the band and Hungry Pussy when V8 jumped on her back. News cameras from a couple of TV stations picked it up then too. The whole scene was played over and over again—at The Cloister everybody said it was like every time a U.S. president got shot.

You could see a more-or-less colourless wraith sidle into the picture behind Hungry Pussy and shuffle toward her. V8 had shed her coat and slippers somewhere. Her bare feet looked silvery, as if they reflected the light.

She wrapped her skinny, pale blue fingers around Hungry Pussy's neck and squeezed. The singer bucked like a horse in a rodeo. V8's legs flailed straight up in the air, but she held on.

Hungry Pussy shook the way a wet dog shakes. She grabbed V8's fingers, but couldn't pull them off. People rushed to help her—the band, backup singers, stage crew, security guys in yellow windbreakers.

"They can't get her to let go," Jimmy McDrool marvelled, watching the TV news.

One guy whacked her over the head with the saxophone. People kicked her, tried to rip her fingers off Hungry Pussy's neck. Somebody pulled out a knife and stabbed at her knuckles. The audience was screaming with rapture. "Yes! Yes!" A great many of the women present would later report that they had experienced orgasm—it was as if they were actually watching somebody get killed on stage. By the time three cops moved into the light, Hungry Pussy's eyeballs were just about squeezed out of their sockets. Her tongue was out. Her head rolled back and forth as if she was unconscious. One of the cops drew his gun and yelled at everybody to back off. He put the muzzle against V8's temple and fired. The bullet went through her head and through the chest of the cop standing on the other side, killing him instantly.

"Do you think Hungry Pussy was dead before they shot V8?" Sister Bernice was sitting with Jimmy McDrool in the TV room. "Or do you think she actually strangled her after?"

"Killed by a dead person with her bare hands," he marvelled.

Nobody claimed V8's body. "Mystery Scrawny Old Lady" was how the media referred to her. Her fingerprints weren't on file. If she had a family, they didn't own up, maybe because they were afraid for their lives. Hungry Pussy fans went on a rampage. A hundred and nineteen people over the age of fifty were killed.

Borofsky put together a tape that included the official footage from the scene as well everything he could download from the instant Web sites where people who had snuck cameras into the concert were eagerly sharing everything they had. He watched it for hours.

Ballantine decided he was losing his mind. If he wasn't, he definitely didn't have any excuse. He decided he was going to stay in his room for the rest of his life, too. Maybe what Banana had was catching.

twenty-two

BUT THERE IS ONLY SO MUCH A man can take. Every time his daughters visited, Ballantine tried a different tactic.

"Oh, Dad's gone deaf!"

"Oh, Dad's gone blind!"

"Oh, Dad's catatonic!"

"Dad has Alzheimer's!"

Nothing worked. They kept coming back.

One was an orthodontist. The other one wasn't. Ballantine could almost tell them apart except the one who wasn't an orthodontist was married to one, so they both talked the talk. And the only thing dental persons talk about is retirement. Having gone through menopause, they were gearing up for the next big adventure—getting ready to die. They both planned to travel a lot.

"Start now!" is what Ballantine wanted to shout, but that week he had lost the ability to speak, the result of a stroke he was trying out on them.

Every time they left, it was like shedding ten years.

He would have been devastated if they didn't come to see him because it made him feel so alive when they left. But he couldn't stand it when they made their precisely timed twenty-five-minute visits because they said such stupid things that it was difficult to maintain the pretense that he was incapable of hearing or speech or sight or whatever. He considered morbid incontinence. If he started shitting himself, maybe it would do the trick.

He doubted it. Today he was trying out a few basic death throes.

"Oh, Dad's not going to be with us much longer."

Too fucking much longer.

Since his door was locked and there had been no response to their knocking, they'd had a maintenance man open it, expecting the worst. They got the worst Ballantine could manage—mouth gaping, tongue lolled out one side, eyes rolled back, entirely unresponsive.

"But his heart's still beating," said the daughter who had stuck her finger under his ear to feel his pulse.

"Thank God we got here in time," said the other one.

Maybe if he relaxed and just went with the flow, Ballantine would become so irritated by their presence it would carry him over the final hurdle into actual death.

He'd decided he was ready to kick off during the Hungry Pussy wrangle when he couldn't figure out whether they should execute her or they shouldn't. When somebody as despicable as Hungry Pussy left open the possibility of redeeming value, everything was to be treasured—polio germs, AIDS, ethnic-cleansing genocidal murderers.

"Look! Dad's having a bowel movement!"

He felt one of them take his hand. "That's wonderful! His internal systems haven't shut down completely." She patted his hand. She put her lips near his ear. "Good for you," she whispered.

Clearly she was insane.

What with guests like V8 starting to freelance, and with John Dillinger and Fastrack and Speed up to all sorts of shady dealings on the international scene, and Borofsky snooping around, Ballantine decided it was as good a time as any.

The next Saturday, a funeral was slated for one in the afternoon. The penguins in their striped trousers and black jackets were early as usual when they wheeled the star of the show, made up and costumed, into the Memorial Chapel, and had nipped across the street for a couple of beers before the service.

As soon as they disappeared, Ballantine pushed a gurney alongside the coffin, tugged and rolled the stiff out on to it, and closed the lid. It wasn't easy. Getting the stiff into his bed was strenuous, too, and Ballantine was dripping with sweat when he put on the stiff's black-rimmed glasses, the perfect disguise, and took a seat in the lounge at the end of the hall. From there he had an unimpeded view of the elevators and the door to his room except he couldn't see anything through the glasses, not even his hand, and had to look over the top of the frames to watch his daughters arrive yattering to each other and knock on his door and go in, still yattering.

Then, "Oh, Dad's having one of his spells."

Then, "Gasp! He's not having a spell. He's—"

"He's—"

Roaring into the hall, they shout for an attendant. A nurse. A doctor. They are hysterical and dazed. They phone their families. Their grief is profound.

Sitting in the sunny lounge, Ballantine is moved to tears to realize how much they miss him.

Which he will realize any minute now.

He looks at his watch.

"What the hell?"

What the fuck?

What in Christ are they doing in there?

Where's the screaming and weeping?

Twenty-five minutes after entering the room they came out. "So long, Dad," they called. "See you next week."

They got on the elevator. The doors closed.

"Of all the fucking…"

"Of all the fucking…"

Ballantine had a feeling he was repeating himself. He couldn't help it.

"Of all the fucking…"

He tried to figure out—what? He couldn't even figure out what he was trying to figure out. Nothing made any sense no matter how he fucking looked at it, so he might as well stop trying to figure it out. And the instant he realized that, he felt distinctly relieved. It was as if he had arrived at an understanding, a conclusion, a philosophy. How could he sum it up? This way: He really was out of his fucking mind.

"I really am out of my fucking mind," he said. "So now what?"

The question hung there, floating at eye level. *So now what?*

Maybe that was the cataclysmic question, the ultimate question. Maybe it was the question of the cosmos. Maybe the answer was the answer to everything, the purest distillation of wisdom, knowledge, intelligence, understanding, of—holy shit!

The answer pushed through the clutter.

And once he knew the answer, it turned out he was wrong about the question. It wasn't an abstraction. It was straightforward. It was even bald-headed. It asked, "So what are you going to do with the stiff in your bed, you dickhead?"

He couldn't just leave it there for the staff to remove. Then Dixon wouldn't even have to come up with some flimsy pretext like a cold to get rid of him. He could be got rid of for a sound technical reason. He was dead.

In the Memorial Chapel the service was starting. Half a dozen guests were present and an equal number of family. As the Duty Rev began, there was muttering among the family members. One spoke quietly to the Duty Rev. The Duty Rev spoke quietly to one of the penguins. The penguin opened the coffin.

There were strangled cries. The Duty Rev flipped through his DayTimer. "Are you sure this is the right day?" As the penguins waddled around the coffin flapping their arms and examining the emptiness from every angle, the Duty Rev tried again. "Are you sure this is the right residential facility?"

An attendant was summoned to lead the way to the loading dock where four stiffs were waiting to be picked up.

"My goodness!" the Duty Rev said to comfort the family members. The family members shook their heads. None of these was theirs. The only thing the guests knew was that in the old days when hearses waited in the lot with their engines running, stiffs disappeared. Now that Fastrack was in the replacement carcass business and there were a lot more stiffs than there were departed guests, things didn't run anywhere near as smoothly.

The Duty Rev led everyone to the administration office. They had hardly left the loading dock when Ballantine pushed the gurney through the swinging doors and over to the stacked corpses. If everything else about this operation had been as simple as it was to roll the stiff on to this pile, it would have been a snap. Ballantine was gratefully sucking in the fresh air when he saw something at the far end of the parking lot.

Not something, someone.

Someone past where the hearses used to wait, way down where the visitors parked.

Borofsky!

Ballantine whipped out the black-framed glasses and put them on. Borofsky vanished. So did everything else. Ballantine slid the glasses down to peek over the tops. Borofsky had his back turned. He was hunched over. As if he didn't want Ballantine to recognize him, to know he'd been spying on him. As if he didn't want Ballantine to know what he'd seen.

He just saw me dump a stiff!

It was time to get the hell out of there. Hurrying through the swinging doors, he looked over the tops of the glasses again. Borofsky was coming this way. Coming to get him!

Ballantine had never been much of a runner, and this wasn't much of a run. Around one corner. Around another corner. He heard the swinging doors on the loading dock open and shut. Down a long corridor. Actually it wasn't a long corridor, it just felt like one. He kept looking for an open door, a room he could duck into. Now he could hear footsteps behind him. Not the rubber-soled *sritch* of staff footsteps, but the solid, determined footsteps of a police officer in hot pursuit.

He ran past the social workers' offices. Past the financial counsellors' offices. Past the Memorial Chapel. He stopped. He ran back. The Memorial Chapel was empty. But there was a coffin at the front. Empty. He climbed in. He pushed the dark-framed eyeglasses up his nose. He crossed his arms on his breast. He closed his eyes.

Borofsky's footsteps came nearer along the corridor. Ballantine had never heard such determined footsteps. Nearer they came. Nearer. Borofsky was at the open door of the Memorial Chapel.

He kept on going. The sound of his footsteps diminished, a long, slow tick at a time. Ballantine didn't move. It might be a trap. He was concentrating so hard on listening for Borofsky to circle around and sneak up on him that he didn't hear the *sritchy* footsteps of a secretary from the administration office. She had been pretty sure the people who had suddenly materialized at her desk yelling about funerals and missing bodies were nuts, but you couldn't be too careful. So, before informing a higher authority, she told them to wait right there. Then she checked the Memorial Chapel.

Just as she thought. They were nuts. There was a corpse in the coffin waiting for the show to get rolling.

Ballantine had almost decided the coast was clear

when he heard the racket of the mourners and penguins rushing back to the Memorial Chapel and decided the wisest course was to lie still and see what happened.

Expressions of pleasure. Exhalations of relief. Everything was as it was supposed to be. The corpse, with its heavy, dark-rimmed glasses, was in the place of honour. The penguins raised their eyebrows at one another and discreetly shrugged. After a moment in silent communion with the departed, the Duty Rev turned to the assembly and raised a consoling hand. "Please," he said, "join in prayer for our beloved friend."

Ballantine thought it was boring. It always was when the only speaker was a Duty Rev, especially a Duty Rev who had never laid eyes on the deceased until that very minute. But he could hardly get up and slip out while everybody had their eyes closed in prayer. He'd have to wait until the end and everybody left.

When the end came—shit! He'd forgotten. Everybody didn't leave. Everybody stayed right where they were, watching the two penguins move forward to close the coffin. The mourners watched them go about their long-practised task. They watched them flick the catch and grip the edges of the lid. They watched them slowly lower it.

They watched the corpse's arms shoot up like pistons and push it back.

They watched the penguins, unused to obstructions, press down.

They watched the corpse's arms stiffen, pushing back harder.

The penguins pressed harder still, putting their shoulders into it.

The corpse whapped his head up and down against the pillow, trying to increase his leverage.

Then the coffin pitched off the stand, hit the floor, and Ballantine tumbled out on to the carpet.

"Jesus!" a family member said.

"Jesus Fucking Christ!"

The heavy, dark-framed glasses had fallen off in the spill, and Ballantine was trying desperately to crawl toward the exit at the back of the chapel.

"What did you think you were doing, you fucking old fuck!"

"You fucking sicko!"

Perhaps the yelling had drawn Borofsky back. Perhaps he had simply decided to retrace his steps. In any event, he was just approaching the Memorial Chapel when Ballantine puffed out the door. Ballantine smiled wanly. He tried to look as if he was on urgent business.

"Ballantine!"

Peremptory. Sharp.

Ballantine stopped. "Yeah?"

"This doesn't have to go any further, okay?"

What in the world did he mean? But okay.

"Good," he said. "Yes. I agree."

"I really don't smoke any more. That one you saw me having out there—it was the first one I've had in a—in a—"

Ballantine staggered. "Fine," was all he could think to say. "Fine."

"I appreciate it."

Borofsky set off toward the back of the building. Two or three of the mourners bumped Ballantine roughly as they passed, but it didn't register on him. Instead he yelled, "Hey!"

This time it was Borofsky's turn to stop.

Ballantine held his arms wide, a gesture of utter incomprehension. "Like, who am I gonna tell that you had a cigarette?"

Borofsky laughed. "You really don't understand guilt, do you?"

twenty-three

THERE HADN'T BEEN A consignment for weeks. The traffic was going in the other direction. "Though I guess," said Mt. Rushmore, "it depends on your point of view."

He and Ballantine were at the sunroom window, watching guests who were being moved out mill around. Those who could mill. Some just slumped on the curb, waiting for rides to their next destination. There had always been a living outflow—for illness, failure to pay, default by insurance companies—but there was a different quality to it now. The guests getting moved out could pay, they just couldn't pay enough. The crowd seemed confused by the moving vans that kept pulling into the semicircular drive, honking their airhorns to edge through. The vans were filled with the belongings of new residents—"not guests," Mt. Rushmore emphasized—moving into the top floors, which were being turned into condominium units. Walls were being knocked down to make spacious apartments, kitchens were being added. Some of these new residents were young. Some were so young that they had little children who scampered through the Concourse in noisy whirlwinds. Guests who complained were taken aside by special placement representatives working out of the administration offices and told the guests had brought it on themselves. They were told that if they didn't like it, they could get out.

"Where does it end?" Ballantine asked.

"When the market peaks, and it's got a long way to go," said Fastrack, who sidled up carrying a box of arrow-root cookies. "That's why I was looking for you. I wanted to show my appreciation."

"For what?" There was something about Fastrack that always made Mt. Rushmore's head ache as if someone was screwing bolts into his skull. The discomfort often caused him to dispense with civility.

"Appreciation because, as of this morning, thanks to the boiler room having mortgaged and remort-gaged and resold and remortgaged the third and fourth mortgages to eager buyers all over the world, The Cloister has reached an evaluation of sixty billion dollars."

"What the fuck are you talking about?"

"We live in the most expensive piece of real estate on earth."

"So? We don't own it."

"What has that got to do with anything?" Fastrack said. "What *does* have to do with something is that it's thanks to you, Ballantine, I was able to accomplish this, and I want to do something for you in return." He held out the box. "Have an arrowroot cookie."

"Thanks," said Ballantine.

Fastrack's jaw dropped. "You're eating it!"

"Why did you give it to me?"

"So you'd have it!"

"I can't have my cookie and eat it too?"

"That's fucking good," said Mt. Rushmore. "Pardon me while I write that down."

Ballantine squinted at Fastrack. "So what was I supposed to do with the arrowroot cookie you gave me, keep it?"

"Not exactly."

"Why would he want to keep it?" said Mt. Rushmore.

"I said not exactly."

"Then what exactly?"

"You'll see." Fastrack marched out of the sunroom.

"You know how in prison, cigarettes are used as currency?" Fastrack said to John Dillinger.

"No," said John Dillinger.

"But nobody in here smokes any more. So I suggest we use arrowroot cookies as currency."

"Why not just use money?"

"You'll see," said Fastrack.

Fastrack settled on the sofa beside Harry the Hat. "It is tradition. Incarcerated people use substitute currency. For instance, I'll give you three arrowroot cookies for—"

"I don't want one arrowroot cookie," Harry the Hat said. "I hate arrowroot cookies."

"You don't eat them. I'm not giving them to you to eat. I'm giving them to you in payment for something so you can spend them on something else. If somebody has something you want, offer them a couple of arrowroot cookies. Eventually it replaces money."

Harry the Hat slid lower on the sofa. He didn't take his eyes off the cartoon channel.

"You'll see," said Fastrack.

Before the arrowroot cookie panic, arrowroot cookies were everywhere in The Cloister. Guests left them out for other guests to share. Visitors brought them as gifts because guests didn't need anything that was inedible, and most edible things the guests couldn't digest. Arrowroot cookies were the world's most digestible foodstuff. But none of the guests helped themselves to the open boxes all over The Cloister. Why would they when they had arrowroot cookies of their own, all they'd ever need?

Sister Bernice briefed the executive committee on the roots of the arrowroot cookie panic. "Nobody can quite describe the flavour of an arrowroot cookie," she began, "except to say it tastes like an arrowroot cookie." Nothing else tastes like it. It is possible that arrowroot cookies taste like arrowroot, but nobody has any idea what arrowroot tastes like or even if it exists. It may be just a name somebody came up with for a particularly flavourless flavour to make it sound more appealing than saying it tasted like absolutely nothing, a logically treacherous notion.

Sweet? Yes and no. Texture—transitory. From sawdusty to mush in an instant.

"Nothing else known to science," said Sister Bernice, offering a box around but not finding any takers, "turns to mush as quickly. There is a substantial school of thought that claims arrowroot cookies are so easy to digest because they are predigested, and then dehydrated for ease of shipping and storage."

It sounded plausible. Everybody was prepared to believe anything disgusting about arrowroot cookies. They were humiliating. They were clear evidence that guests' lives had come full circle. They had been reduced to infancy. All that was left was to no longer exist.

"One of the reasons it's so easy to get staff to work in these palliative care units," Chardonnay explained to Ballantine, "where you might think there is nothing but turmoil and grief, is that the patients shit pure arrowroot cookie. Having to clean them up every twenty minutes is not as unpleasant as many assume."

Pretty well the only people who could still stand to eat them were the gagas, but once they became a valued currency, if a gaga had some, there was somebody around sharp enough to screw them out of it. It isn't hard to screw a gaga out of anything, but until Fastrack's scheme took hold, gagas never had much of anything worth getting screwed out of.

The only way guests could keep track of the exchange rate for arrowroot cookies was through Fastrack's Web site or by looking at the Big Board he had set up in the Concourse. Since the rate fluctuated moment to moment, guests were either stuck to their computers or forced to sit for hours in the Concourse. Being out of touch could mean the loss of life savings as well as any good or chattel put up as collateral to borrow money to purchase arrowroot cookies.

Guests began sneaking across the street to the supermarket and buying all the arrowroot cookies in stock at the going rate for arrowroot cookies on the retail market and returning to The Cloister multimillionaires at the going rate for arrowroot cookies on the Big Board. Guests desperate to get hold of arrowroot cookies were prepared to sell anything they had—their blue-chip stocks, retirement savings bonds, furs, jewellery. When they ran out of everything else, they sold the furnishings in their rooms, but since the beds and dressers and chairs didn't technically belong to them, they were forced to let them go at extremely reduced rates. Soon they were selling the rooms on the black market operated by the special placement representatives in the administration offices.

Wild fluctuations in the price of arrowroot cookies prompted efforts to corner the market and to identify hoarders. For the first time there was violent crime inside The Cloister. Guests' rooms were broken into, drawers were dumped, pillows slashed, closets looted, ceiling panels pulled down. Stashes of arrowroot cookies that guests were depending on to get them through the coming difficult years were stolen. Guests travelled the halls in groups for fear of being waylaid, beaten senseless, and having their arrowroot cookies snatched. But what chance did even a large band of decrepit old people have against a marauding band of decrepit old people armed with pepper spray and automatic weapons? Two or three guests with bullet wounds were transported to hospital every day. The terror peaked on movie night when masked bandits turned on the lights in the rec room and held the audience hostage until all their arrowroot cookies were handed over. They threatened to shoot one hostage an hour until this was done, and to prove they were serious, they shot Harry the Hat.

When innocent guests at The Cloister began to value arrowroot cookies more than their lives or the lives of others, Sister Bernice drew the line. For the first time the executive committee gave serious consideration to knocking off one of its own members. There was usually no shortage of in-house nominations, usually from dining-room tablemates or next-door neighbours objecting to noises or smells. But there was something more to Fastrack's nomination, and he fought against it with all the energy he could muster. He spoke so eloquently and passionately that everyone was surprised by the eighteen-to-one vote in favour of popping him. Sister Bernice, who had imagined she was registering no more than a protest vote, was anguished to think seventeen others might have done the same. There was no way that destroying the lives and happiness of those who lived in The Cloister was comparable to what other candidates had done. And Fastrack hadn't done it to ruin their lives. He had done it for their own good, just as selling The Cloister over and over on the international market provided financing for executive actions. Their ruined lives were a mere side effect, unintended, just as it had been unintended that the top five floors were now inhabited by young people with big plans and screaming children.

Everyone who cast a ballot in favour of eliminating Fastrack was horrified and spoke vigorously against the result. But since there was, for purposes of fairness and to prevent interference, no interface between the executive committee that voted for elimination and the executives who carried it out, even though they were usually the same people, it was too late. Fastrack was doomed. And a damn good thing, too. The sooner the better. However, because the executives selected to knock Fastrack off had qualms about the outcome of the vote, they decided not to do anything, but they agreed with Mt. Rushmore that if Fastrack got run over by a bus, it would be no skin off their asses.

Fastrack said that if everybody only understood how the market worked, the committee wouldn't be wasting its time talking about eliminating him because everybody would know he had nothing to do with it. What guided the market was an invisible hand.

Ballantine wondered if it was the same invisible hand that caused the cable to snap when the giant crane that had taken down the sign over the front entrance that said "The Cloister" was raising brushed aluminum letters, each six feet high, that spelled out "Dixon Renaissance Tower" and the W fell and crushed the life out of Fastrack, who had been on his way to the supermarket across the street to check on the arrowroot cookie situation.

After stumbling blindly for a couple of days while they tried to calculate the worth of arrowroot cookies in the absence of Fastrack, people went back to using cash and seldom mentioned the arrowroot cookie episode, other than to say that they couldn't understand how anybody would be foolish enough to get caught up in anything that stupid.

twenty-four

HE SOUNDED VERY ANGRY.

"This is a real piss-off!"

Mourners tensed.

"What is the matter with you people?"

Screaming Maureen's late husband blamed them for everything.

The Duty Rev glared at the ceiling. He pointed an index finger upward. "Is there some way we can turn that off?"

"Go turn your fucking self off," said the voice from beyond the grave.

The Duty Rev opened and closed his mouth a couple of times. "This isn't funny," he said.

"No fucking kidding!" bellowed the voice.

"I'm going to see about this." The Duty Rev stalked up the aisle and out the door.

Sister Bernice turned to Ballantine. "Trouble in paradise?"

"I had a good thing going until you people let that dried-up old cunt die," said the voice.

"Wilf—"

It was Screaming Maureen.

"Wilf?" said Sister Bernice.

"Wilf?" whispered Mt. Rushmore from the next pew.

"Wilf, it is I."

It was powerful—seeing Screaming Maureen lying in

the coffin at the front of the Memorial Chapel while her voice, strong, reverberant, came from the afterlife.

Ballantine looked at Mt. Rushmore. "'It is I.' I guess they do talk like that up there."

"Go to hell, Maureen!" Her late husband's voice was bitter. "Nobody wants you here. Go to hell!"

"I told you." Screaming Maureen didn't sound even slightly ruffled. "I just wanted you to fuck off and leave me alone. I didn't care about your love life. I didn't care if you got a blow job every five minutes. I just didn't want to hear. But, no, you had to be hurtful."

"You stinking old—"

"It was so unnecessary."

"I didn't think there was fighting in heaven," Ballantine whispered.

"Maybe they're not in heaven," said Sister Bernice.

"They must be," said Mt. Rushmore. "All those blow jobs."

Anytime Wilf's voice had been heard before, panic had spread, but this time was different. "Calm, but riveted," was how Mt. Rushmore described the mourners at the funeral on "News & Views Roundup."

"Everybody agreed with me," Screaming Maureen continued. "You were just mouthing off to make me feel bad."

"You deserved it, you—" The voice rose sharply. "What's that?!"

"What does it look like?" replied the late Screaming Maureen.

"No!"

"No what?" said Ballantine. He stared at Screaming

Maureen lying in front of them as if the corpse might give him a clue.

"I don't believe this," said Sister Bernice.

"What don't you believe?" said Mt. Rushmore.

"Anything."

"Me neither."

Around the chapel, people were asking their neighbours what they thought was going on, asking them whether they believed their ears, telling them to shush so they wouldn't miss anything.

"It won't do anything." Screaming Maureen's late husband's voice sounded quite superior. "We're immortal here. Or didn't you know that?"

"Oh, I heard," said Screaming Maureen.

"So fuck off, all right? Please, okay? Just leave me a— No! No! Please, I—"

The silence continued for some time. Nobody moved.

"She pulled the pin?" Mt. Rushmore asked at last.

"She had a hand grenade?"

"I don't know. Maybe it was a sword."

"The hand grenade in the afterlife." Sister Bernice sighed happily.

The Duty Rev swept back in leading an attendant. "Is it still happening?" he asked, looking at the ceiling.

Black-Eyed Susan sounded entirely bewildered. "Is what still happening?"

"The voices." The Duty Rev pointed straight up.

"Voices?"

Something about Mt. Rushmore's voice saying "Voices?" caught the attendant's attention. Mt. Rushmore widened his eyes and tapped his temple. The attendant looked at the Duty Rev, who was still looking expectantly at the ceiling.

"Reverend Woowoo," Black-Eyed Susan whispered. All the mourners nodded at the attendant, who backed up a couple of steps, then hustled out of the chapel.

The Duty Rev stiffened. He threw back his shoulders and tugged his robe closed. "I'll proceed then," he said, moving back to the lectern and staring narrowly around the room, "shall I?"

Borofsky fell in beside Ballantine at the rear of the chapel. "What the hell was that all about?"

"I didn't know you were sitting back here," said Ballantine.

"Don't give me that shit. What was going on?"

"Do you think it was a hand grenade?"

"Hand grenade?"

Ballantine laughed. "If somebody got murdered in heaven, it would be the perfect murder wouldn't it? No weapon would be found. No clues. Maybe not even a victim. You didn't know about Screaming Maureen's husband?" Ballantine was genuinely surprised.

"What about him?"

"That voice—anyway his voice—I can't believe you've been around here so much and haven't heard him. Or heard about him."

"You're telling me somebody wasn't just fucking the minister over?"

"We've tried electronic scanning. Swept the place for bugs."

"Bullshit."

"Ask anybody. It's kind of creepy. Except—"

"Except what?"

"Except it's so entertaining."

Borofsky followed Ballantine into a sunroom and sat on the footstool directly in front of Ballantine's armchair.

"That's your idea of perfection?"

Ballantine looked confused. "Sorry?"

"Perfection. Heaven. Where you can commit the perfect crime and nobody can track you down." Borofsky sounded very angry. Ballantine wondered whether his job was becoming too much for him.

Ballantine rested his head against the chairback and looked out the window. "It doesn't sound like the heaven I learned about in Sunday School. I don't know. But then I know less every day. It's the one good thing about my life."

"I wouldn't know," Borofsky said, and began telling Ballantine what he knew.

He had the "Notable Passings" from The Cloister's newsletters, none of which involved individuals who had lived in The Cloister, or had any connection with anyone who had ever lived in The Cloister yet, for some reason, their passings were of interest to guests in The Cloister. The only thing they had in common was that they had all died unexpectedly and violently. He also had the videotapes Minimum Max had made of his sermons as head of the Church of the Second Coming of Christ, Assassin, covering much the same ground. He'd tracked down twenty-one little explosive devices found in the fourteenth tee at the Rosewell Golf Club after the chairman of the Big One Confederated Bank had the living shit blown right out of him. Borofsky had found them in the unlabelled bottom drawer of a filing cabinet containing nothing else but microfiches of pre-1943 departmental recruiting and training manuals. He also had the Glock nine-millimetre automatic pistol that the department had issued to Amy Wheatcroft. It had been found beside the weird suitcase gun used to shoot Miles Concannon's nuts off. Coincidentally, it had fired the shots that had killed three men involved in smuggling stolen cars out of, and Asians into, the country.

"You never heard of the Gunfight at the OK Intermodal Shipping Terminal." It wasn't a question.

"Was that a movie?" Ballantine asked.

And he had watched his taped multimedia medley of V8 strangling Hungry Pussy twenty-five times.

"I gave her an answer for the crossword puzzle she tried to hide under her pillow."

Ballantine was nonplussed.

"It was 'Kemo sabe'. How come you decided to shoot Miles Concannon's nuts off?"

"What are you talking about?"

"As opposed to killing him?"

Ballantine's thumbs rubbed back and forth against each other. Like twiddling, but entirely involuntary. He didn't used to do it, and then one day he noticed that he sometimes did it, and that he had nothing at all to do with it. A huge smile carried the corners of his face upward.

"You know what I wonder?" He bathed Borofsky in the smile. "I wonder if maybe that was an accident."

"An accident! You guys fuck up, so now we got this

nutless lunatic blowing up massage parlours all over the world!"

"I saw something about those explosions. I had no—"

"No warning. Just boom! So far he's killed eighty people who thought they were just going to sneak in and get a quiet hand job."

Collateral damage. They had worked so hard to avoid it. But here they were, one botched job and innocents were being slaughtered. Christ!

"What?"

"I didn't say anything." Ballantine looked around. For a moment he was almost uncertain where he was.

"I thought you said something about collateral damage."

"Excuse me." Ballantine pushed himself up from the chair. It took quite a long time. "I'm feeling a little ill."

"He said what?" Mt. Rushmore was so surprised he poured his whole cup of tea over the salt and pepper shakers.

Ballantine watched tea flood toward him across the table. He built a dam of paper napkins.

"Say it again, what he said."

"He said, 'Anyway, I'm not afraid of you.'"

"He said that!" Mt. Rushmore raised the cup to his lips. Then he held it out and looked into it. He turned it upside down and shook it a couple of times. "I thought I just poured myself some tea," he said.

twenty-five

THE BUSES HAD BEEN COMING, sometimes two or three a day, for a few weeks. Ballantine and Mt. Rushmore had fiddled the list to make sure they got on the same one. Theirs was due this morning. Ballantine was packed—all he had was a gym bag—and was watching out the sunroom window. He was unspeakably weary, the way he felt after lifting that heavy coil of bungee cord to the roof parapet like an idiot when he was murdering Asshole No. 2. He could hear blood vessels bursting in his temples.

When he opened his eyes, he watched a hearse move up the street and into the driveway. It was glass on all four sides, with fluted black columns at each corner. The wheels had wooden spokes. He saw that the departed was Sister Bernice. He'd forgotten her funeral was today. Until he saw himself reflected in the hearse's windows, he'd forgotten he'd dressed for the occasion in a pearl-grey suit with white satin lapels that he couldn't remember ever seeing before. He couldn't remember the grey derby with the wide, white satin band either. He'd had no idea Mt. Rushmore could drive a team of horses, but there he was in a black topper up on the box. The four horses were tall and black, their coats so shiny they reflected the sky. Black plumes nodded between their ears. Sister Bernice reclined on the coffin's pillows, looking glamorous. When he rapped on the glass, she blew him so many kisses he could tell she was happy he was there.

Then the band started and Mt. Rushmore clicked his tongue to get the horses moving. It was a brass band, ten or a dozen men in red trousers and gold shirts and caps like railway conductors used to wear, only red and gold.

Ballantine had never heard music as mournful and slow.

The only cemetery near enough to reach on foot was an old Jewish one with yellowed stucco walls, its gate boarded and padlocked. Concertina wire looped along the tops of the walls and over the gabled entry. As they approached it, the band split in two and lined the sides of the street.

"We turnin' her loose!" the musicians called to one another.

"Amen!"

"Turn her loose!"

"What town we in?"

"What difference it makes?"

"Look, she ain't even dead! She wavin'!"

"Lord have mercy."

The trumpeter played "Taps" as Mt. Rushmore hauled hard left and the horses sidled around, their hooves striking sparks on the pavement. He gave the reins a flip and the hearse came back through the band.

"We turned her loose, but here she is again."

"Maybe the cemetery wouldn't take her!"

"I told you she wasn't dead!"

"Old lady, she just out for a ride!"

"None of our business! Drummer, pull out that rag!"

The snare drummer tugged the handkerchief out of the snares, and his roll crackled off the cemetery wall. Mt. Rushmore tipped his hat.

The trumpeter shouted, "I'm goin' to hold up my big ol' hand—"

"Do that!"

"—and when I brings it down—"

"Lord have mercy!"

"Yes!"

"—we goin' to cast off our sadness!"

"Yeeeow!"

"Cast it off!"

"We goin' to ramble!"

Children spun around Ballantine, high-stepping with him. Sister Bernice had climbed out of the coffin and was pressing her hands against the glass, rotating her hips to the music, rolling her head from shoulder to shoulder. Ballantine was astonished—he knew so many people lining the curb. People he hadn't seen since the army, some not since high school. They laughed and called out, and he did little pirouettes, holding on to the brim of his hat with his pinky raised. Lots of people were dressed in costumes—clowns, pirates, who knows what all. They shimmied up to Ballantine and strutted along. Prostitutes came out of the bars, calling him "Sugar" and planting smudgy kisses on his cheeks. Drunks imitated his joyful step. Helicopters flew overhead, and Ballantine imagined the wonderful pictures they'd be getting for the news that night. The helicopters circled the hearse, then zipped away like dragonflies in the direction of The Cloister. And look—here were his daughters! They sashayed out, one on either side of him. He had never seen them so playful. They told him their mother would be along any minute. He said she'd have no trouble catching up. Customers he'd sold fruits and vegetables to forty years ago gave him thumbs-up. Imagine that! He had never seen Sister Bernice dance before—she sure could shake her ass! Nobody could hear the music and stand still, and it took him awhile to separate the sound of gunfire from the sound of the band. When he finally did, he realized he'd been hearing it for some time.

As they turned the corner, a helicopter swung into view and raked The Cloister with machine guns. Fire was returned from the upper floors where the young people and their children were putting up a stiff resistance, but the rest of the building was silent. Flames licked out of shattered windows. Now there were three or four helicopters shooting at everything. Ballantine could read "The Concannon Way" on their sides, and under that, "My Way or the Die Way."

The marching band had disappeared—probably taken cover. Ballantine's daughters must have run for it, too. The crowd that lined the streets was nowhere to be seen. Ballantine wondered why Mt. Rushmore hadn't stopped the horses, and hurried forward to yell at him, but Mt. Rushmore was lying on the driver's seat, the bottom of his face shot away. Sister Bernice banged on the glass, shouting at Ballantine to get her out of there, but before he could a helicopter opened up and she was thrown in a bloody heap across the coffin.

Ballantine's heart was pounding so hard he thought it would break his ribs. He felt cold. When he looked now, the only things in front of The Cloister were the bus waiting for him and the line of moving vans waiting to unload. That's all, except for the police officer walking up the drive. Strangest looking cop Ballantine had ever seen, like one of the clown people from the parade. The uniform was stretched to bursting. The fly didn't come anywhere near closing, and a white belly ballooned over it. Now Ballantine saw it was a policewoman. She stopped outside the sunroom window. Her wig was bright red and stuck out in all directions. She smiled at him, her teeth smeared red from her lipstick. She beckoned. Come out here.

Ballantine ran. He'd been running a lot lately, though it didn't seem to be doing him any good. Out of the sunroom, across the Concourse, past the reception desk, down the corridor, through the swinging doors that led to the loading docks. Moving vans were lined up back here, too. He'd had no idea. He crossed the parking lot—maybe he could hijack a hearse! But there weren't any. Hearses had stopped waiting ages ago. If he got clear of the building he could—what? Goddamned if he knew. Flee on the subway? Flee what? A clown that had escaped from his daydream?

What a moron.

He'd go back and find Mt. Rushmore, and they'd get on the bus and let themselves be taken—Jesus! There she was! Waddling toward him. She had her gun out. It looked exactly like V8's gun. She was pointing it at him and yelling, "Stop right there, you son of a bitch!"

He started running again. But as fast as he could run, she could waddle faster. He could have saved himself a lot of effort if he'd just waited for her.

When Borofsky came charging around the building, they were just starting across the bridge that led downtown.

"Hey!" he yelled. It was the screwiest thing he'd ever seen. An old man who could barely move was being chased by a joke cop who could barely move. And then he recognized the cop. Holy shit! It was Amy Wheatcroft.

And she had her gun back!

"Hey!"

He had almost caught up when she stopped. "Get away!" She rounded on Borofsky. "Stay away!"

Departmental issue. Glock nine-millimetre.

"You crazy fucking—" Borofsky was out of breath. "Where'd you get that gun?"

"It's my gun."

"Where did you fucking get it?"

"You're not the only one who knows his way around the force."

"How did—?" Borofsky pointed at Ballantine, who had stopped running when everybody else did, then at her, and back again.

"When you started sniffing around, I thought you might be on to something, so I did a little detective work. It's not as if you don't leave a trail."

"It was that big a deal?"

"I loved this gun. My gun. I loved my gun. I loved being a police officer. It made me feel beautiful and strong. I could hardly wait for the day I'd get a chance to use my gun to shoot a bad guy. It was a long time coming." She jacked the slide and aimed at Ballantine's nose.

Looking into the enormous barrel, Ballantine thought how perfect it all was. How peaceful he felt. As close to perfect peace as he ever had. Or as he ever would again because Borofsky dropped to one knee and yelled, "Drop that fucking gun! Drop that fucking gun or I'll shoot! Freeze, asshole!"

He scrabbled at his ankle. Then he scrabbled at his other ankle. Then he shouted, "Where's my fucking gun?" Had he left it in the car? In the glove compartment? He hoped it wasn't lying on the seat. He leapt up and flung himself on Amy Wheatcroft's back. Almost. His leap only took him halfway. Then he stopped cold.

Because Amy Wheatcroft had stopped cold. "What's with my gun?" she said. Her voice was plaintive. "It's jammed." She shook it a couple of times, pointed it at Ballantine's nose and tried again.

Borofsky couldn't believe it. Glocks never jammed. That's why so many police forces used them.

"Is there something wrong?" Ballantine sounded genuinely concerned.

Borofsky grabbed Amy Wheatcroft by the hair. "Give me that fucking thing," he demanded, but instead she threw it. It hit Ballantine on the temple and he fell backwards. "Now get the fuck out of here, you crazy fucking..." Borofsky pushed her toward the other end of the bridge. "Go on! Fuck off!" And she waddled away.

Borofsky looked at the gun. Fucking amazing. He threw it as far as he could and watched it curve down into the river.

"I thought for a minute I was a goner," Ballantine said as Borofsky helped him to his feet.

"You just about were."

"Oh, well," Ballantine said, and began limping back toward the idling bus.

"Where's it taking you?"

"Who knows," Ballantine said. "They just circle the city until they find a place that's got a room. But there aren't any rooms. Whenever there's a room, it's turned into a condo."

"So you just keep—"

"Circling."

"Where have you guys been?" Mt. Rushmore was standing at the bus door. "This thing isn't going to wait forever." He had Ballantine's gym bag. "You left this in the sunroom."

"We had a little business to attend to," Borofsky said.

"Yeah," said Ballantine. He turned to Borofsky and took a deep breath. "So I guess that's it."

Borofsky shook his head. "For you, maybe."

Mt. Rushmore, who was halfway up the steps, leaned down and looked at Borofsky. "Did you just say what I think you said?"

"Maybe," said Borofsky.

"In that case," said Ballantine. He pulled something bundled in a T-shirt out of his gym bag. He unwrapped it and handed it to Borofsky.

"What the fuck is this?"

"V8's gun."

"But I just threw it in the river." He looked closely. It was engraved with Amy Wheatcroft's name and her badge number. In place of the "m" in Amy there was a little heart.

"We had a few copies made," Ballantine said. "Some of them weren't too reliable. This is the real one."

Mt. Rushmore clumped on up the steps. "If our experience is anything to go by, it'll come in handy."

"Next year, when you retire," said Ballantine.